TAILGATES & HEARTACHES

LOCALS #2

HALEY RHOADES

This is a work of fiction. Names, characters, businesses, places, events, and incidents are either the products of the author's imagination or used in a fictitious manner. Any resemblance to actual persons, living or dead, or actual events is purely coincidental.

Any trademarks, service marks, product names, or named features are assumed to be the property of their respective owners and are used only for reference. There is no implied endorsement.

Tailgates & Heartaches, The Locals #2
Copyright © 2018 Haley Rhoades
All rights reserved.

Cover Design by Germancreative on Fiverr

eBook ISBN: 978-1-959199-00-7
Paperback ISBN: 978-0-9989590-6-1

 Created with Vellum

ENHANCE YOUR READING

To Enhance Your Reading of Tailgates & Heartaches
read the Trivia Page near the end of the book
prior to opening chapter #1.

No Spoilers-I promise.

1

MADISON

I turn off my playlist opting instead for random radio stations as background noise. The three-hour drive seems longer tonight. My thoughts fly all over the place—I contemplate my past, my present, and my future. I haven't heard a lyric of any songs since they started over an hour ago when I left Athens.

I struggle to process every interaction with Hamilton earlier this evening. My best friend since eighth grade seemed to be much more tonight. I wonder if our friends noticed, and what did he really mean when he said goodbye and I love you?

Did he mean 'I love you best friend'? Or like his extra touches and closeness all evening was he sending me a message? Were we still best friends or are we becoming more?

Once the shock of Hamilton attending the wedding wore off, I expected to be on pins and needles around him—I was not prepared for his actions. He was the same old Hamilton with new touches. When in my proximity, his hands were constantly on me. In the past, he did touch me to offer his support in a friendly manner. Tonight, he played with my loose tendrils, his lips grazed my ear, and he kissed me goodbye telling me he loved me. He didn't hide any of this from our friends at the reception. To further cloud my thoughts, at moments he was friendly while at others he was *more*. I don't know where we stand—to say I am confused by his actions is an understatement.

More. Do I want more? Of course, I do. I need him—*we* need him. He's in Chicago or on the road while we're in Columbia. Where do we go from here?

That kiss. Oh my gosh what a goodbye kiss and to me it felt like so much more than a friendly goodbye.

I quickly swat my cheeks to snap out of the lust-filled, hopeful thoughts of Hamilton before returning my hands to the steering wheel. I attempt to focus as I sing along with Imagine Dragons on the radio. The lyrics speak to me. They explain we have no tomorrow without having what we did yesterday. Our past AKA yesterday affects our future AKA our tomorrow. The song is a message, a sign. My past affects every part of my future.

My mind drifts as I remember playing with magnets as a child. When I placed the north-pole of one magnet near the south-pole of another magnet, they attracted each other. But, when I placed two north-poles or two south-poles near each other the magnets repelled one another. It's the whole opposites attract saying come to life. I'm a south-pole magnet while many of my friends are north-pole magnets. We grew up in the small rural town of Athens, Missouri. My friends (north-poles) and the town of Athens (south-pole) attract each other. They are happy to be born, raised, attend school, marry, start a family, and live their entire lives in Athens. Since Athens and I are south-pole magnets we repel one another. In high school, my one goal was to leave town after graduation and never return.

One year has now passed since my high school graduation. I remain in contact with my girlfriends during our Sunday evening phone and video calls. They keep me up-to-date on their lives as well as some of the gossip in Athens. I share about my college classes at the University of Missouri, Alma, and her family. She opened her home to me while I attend classes and is much more than a roommate.

I made only one trip to Athens in the eleven months since I left town—now I hope to visit more often. I miss my friends and find phone calls aren't enough. I long to see them more often and to share everything I've kept from them. The weight of my secret grows heavier with each passing day. I made a promise to myself to meet with Hamilton at the end of this Chicago Cubs season—it's time to tell him *everything*. As it's nearly June now, I have four months to figure out how to explain my actions to the second most important person in my life.

As my car enters the city limits of Columbia, I know my three-hour drive comes to an end. Relief washes over me as I pull in Alma's driveway at just after 2:00 a.m. This drive from Adrian's wedding to her hunky man Winston allowed me to contemplate the past twelve months and plan for the next twelve. My mind seems clearer than it has been in a long time, except for one thing that still haunts me.

Stepping from my car, my tender foot makes contact with a rock on the concrete reminding me I removed my boots an hour into the drive. I grab my cowboy boots from the passenger seat and my small suitcase from the back. Barefoot I carefully tiptoe up the porch steps into our house.

Alma kindly left a lamp on in the front sitting room for my middle of the night return. I take my boots and bag up to my room and change into pajamas before making my way to the kitchen. With Alma's bedroom just off the back and Liberty sleeping soundly in her portable crib in one corner of the kitchen, I quietly place a water and two of Alma's homemade oatmeal raisin cookies on the corner of the counter. I flip off the lights, carefully lift Libby to my chest, and grab my snack. Juggling water, cookies, and my daughter prove a challenge as I head back upstairs. I drop my treats on the hall table before entering the nursery.

Attending the wedding today is my first trip away from Liberty. Although I didn't spend the night, eighteen hours away seems like forever. I slip into the rocker to enjoy a few more moments cuddling her in my arms. I pepper her forehead with kisses and tug on a couple of her springy chestnut curls.

"I saw daddy today," I whisper. "You look so much like him. His hair, his eyes, and his smile made me miss you even more." I attempt to swallow the lump forming in my throat. "He looked so handsome in his western attire. We even danced together. Your daddy is a great dancer."

My long, exciting, and emotional day settles in. Tears well in my eyes, I kiss my daughter one more time before I lay her in the crib, turn on the baby monitor, and head to my bedroom. I want nothing more than to cuddle Libby in my bed tonight—I feel raw. Seeing all eight of my high school friends in Athens today, celebrating Adrian and Winston's wedding, and the mixed signals from Hamilton wore me out emotionally and physically. I long for her sweet baby cuddles to comfort me tonight. I've been up since 5:00 a.m.—it's almost 3:00 a.m. now. Liberty usually wakes around 7:00, so I need to grab sleep while I can. After breakfast, Alma will help me process everything from my long confusing day. With no more strength, sleep engulfs me.

2

MADISON

Shortly after 7:00 a.m., Liberty's soft coos filter through the monitor on my beside table. Although I am exhausted, I need to see her little face. I peek into the crib loving the instant excitement on her face at seeing her mommy. I bid her good morning as I lift her. While I change her diaper, she mumbles around the chubby fist in her mouth. I like to think she is filling me in on her day alone with Alma. I place a kiss on her chubby cheek as we make our way to the kitchen.

Alma sips coffee while reading the Sunday paper in the breakfast nook enjoying the late-May sunlight through the bay window. She smiles at the sight of us then asks what time I got in last night claiming she didn't hear me.

I grab a bottle of formula from the refrigerator, place it in hot water to warm, and grab a diet cola before joining Alma at the table. Liberty continues sucking on her little fist and cooing as I answer Alma. As I take long drinks from my cola, I internally wish the caffeine to rapid-fire into my blood stream. I'm going to need more than one caffeinated beverage this morning.

"I loved the photos you texted me. Adrian was a lovely bride."

"It was..." I search for the perfect word that comes close to describing Adrian's special day. "It was a stress-free, magical day. Simple plans carried out by her large family and friends allowed everyone to enjoy the day.

I enjoy another drink of my diet cola, test Libby's bottle on my wrist, then offer it to her. She sucks the bottle as if she's gone days without eating. Even after two and a half months, I still giggle at the little piglet sounds she makes while eating. I blame her unladylike appetite on her father. I lovingly gaze at her while I continue my conversation with Alma.

"The sun's rays were like a halo behind the barn during the ceremony and just as the vows ended twilight began. The fairy lights inside the barn illuminated perfectly. I'm not sure I want bridesmaids in cowboy boots and a country wedding someday, but I hope it can run as smoothly and everyone enjoy themselves just like Adrian's wedding."

"And Hamilton?" Alma doesn't allow me to ignore the elephant in the room. I'm certain she spotted him in the group photos I texted her.

I share my shock in finding him in the barn before the ceremony. I explain my attempts to busy myself with maid-of-honor duties to avoid him all evening and I share in detail his every word and touch at the reception. Then as Alma furrows her brow, I tell her everything that happened at the stop sign before we drove away from each other into the pitch-black night.

I take a gulp from my beverage waiting for Alma's words of wisdom. In the past twelve months I've benefited from her wealth of knowledge and lessons learned in her sixty-five years of life. She's raised two daughters and a son while active in her church and community, it seems she's experienced it all.

I remove the bottle from Libby's lips with her immediately protesting. "Patience sweetie, patience," I croon as I pat her back in search of a burb from her little belly. Alma and I laugh when the loud belch sounds and I kiss Libby on the cheek before returning the bottle. Alma uses Libby's distraction to ponder all I've shared.

"I don't know Hamilton, except from what you have shared, so I am just spit-balling here." Alma begins. "He's alone and far from home in Chicago. He spends endless hours on busses, on airplanes, and in hotel rooms. He's in the public-eye and commentators are hyper-critical of his performance on the mound. He's a small-town farm boy very far from his element. I'm sure he misses Athens and you." Alma pauses to sip from her coffee mug with its words 'grand-ma's go-go juice'.

"In an unexpected twist of fate, his schedule changed at the last minute, and he was permitted to spend mere hours surrounded by everyone important to him. I bet he didn't plan to constantly touch you, to kiss you, or to confess his love for you. I think the sight of you rekindled his feelings and the brevity of your time together spawned him into action." She fiddles with the corners of her newspaper. "If his feelings for you are like your feelings for him, he may have found himself powerless to fight them. Perhaps the thought of going eleven more months without physically being in your presence drove him to act."

Reaching across the table, Alma squeezes my free hand. "I agree they don't seem the actions of a best friend. I think he has feelings for you. Now what he plans to do going forward, I don't dare speculate. You have two options. You can discuss this with him the next time you speak over the phone, or you can sit back and wait for him to make the next move."

Her words help. I worried I had read more into Hamilton's actions exaggerating them in my mind. Alma interprets the same as I. Where I go from here, I don't know but I have time to contemplate it for a day or two before I speak to him next. For now, my insides are toasty warm with a flicker hope.

3

MADISON

Alma offers to take Liberty for a walk in her stroller with McGee on his leash, while I am on my weekly video call with my girls in Athens. I love that Alma's puppy calmly walks near Libby's stroller. On our first few walks in April, it took both of us to handle the stroller and Alma's ten-month-old, male, mini-chocolate Labradoodle. Among the hundreds of things, she's taught me this year is how to successfully train her puppy McGee.

Promptly at 7:00 p.m. Salem's FaceTime rings and Alma slips with our two little ones out the front door. "Long time no see," She greets in Adrian's absence. I greet my three friends. We animatedly relive yesterday evening's wedding and reception. Savannah asks what we think Adrian and Winston are doing right at this moment—we all agree we don't want to even think about it.

"Speaking of couples doing the nasty, Bethany, I didn't plan to see you on tonight's video call. Shouldn't you be celebrating your first anniversary with Troy right now?" I assumed she'd be on some romantic dinner date with her man spoiling her. The two are very affectionate when in public. Even in high school, I marveled at their constant contact with hands in each other's pockets, arms around each other, and kissing regardless who might see.

A blush quickly creeps up Bethany's neck and face. With her fair-complexion it borders between bright pink and red. "We celebrated before breakfast, in the shower, before our afternoon nap, and just before I drove to Salem's," she confesses proudly. "I wanted to share last night but didn't want to rob Adrian of her moment. She'll be pissed I shared without her here, but I can't keep the secret another minute." She bites her lower lip, smiles, then announces, "We are officially trying to get pregnant!"

Although it's no surprise, we celebrate with our friend. During our junior year of high school, the couple planned to move-in together immediately after graduation, marry, and start a family within a year. Excited to share her news, Bethany fills us in on ovulation calendars, fertility windows, and many other facts that as single women we aren't interested in.

"Bethany, honey," ever-sweet Salem interrupts. "The only thing we need to know from you is the three-day window during which we don't want to visit or even drive by your love shack." Loud laughter fills the air.

"Oh, laugh now Salem," Bethany quips. "your day will come. Your wedding is on the calendar sweetie, so little Latham's won't be far from that." More laughter erupts from all four of us.

When we regain our breath, Salem proceeds to inform me Bethany will be her maid-of-honor for the December wedding. Behind Salem, I notice Savannah and Bethany whispering while glancing at me before whispering some more.

"What are you two rudely whispering about?" I interrupt causing Savannah to elbow Bethany.

"Was last night *really* the first time you've seen Hamilton since he was drafted?" Bethany blurts. "I mean except for saying hi to him after his Major League debut at Wrigley Field?"

My three friends stare at me through my laptop screen. "Yes. I said goodbye to him from his mother's driveway the day he left for Des Moines. Memphis and I spent an hour with him after his first game pitching for the I-Cubs. You were all with me when we attended another I-Cubs game. Then Alma and her family joined me for fifteen minutes after his Wrigley debut. Why?"

"Seriously?" Bethany taunts. "Did you think we were blind last night at Adrian's reception?" She crosses her arms in front of her chest. I imagine she is also tapping her toe annoyed at me.

Salem jumps in, "Hamilton couldn't keep his eyes off you the entire night. Something is up—I think you have been holding out on us."

I play dumb in hopes they will describe what they witnessed and what they believe it meant. I can use all the help I can get on this topic.

"Madison, you know I tend not to weigh in on relationship crap," Savannah chimes in. "I personally witnessed two incidents that his lips brushed your ear and temple. He's never done that in public before that I know of. In fact, with all of his high school dating, I've never witnessed public displays of affection from him. He didn't hold their hands, put his arm around them, whisper in their ear, or kiss them in public. He held your hand last night, he placed his hand at the small of your back, he kissed your temple, whispered in your ear, and held you tight against him while the two of you danced." She shrugs. "It caught me off guard. When these two mentioned it, I knew it wasn't just my imagination."

"So, you can see why we might think the two of you have met sometime in the off-season. There was a new chemistry between you that wasn't your normal best friend interactions." Bethany urges. "I'll only ask once and then I'll let it go. Did the two of you get together this past winter?"

Here I go again. In keeping my pregnancy from Hamilton, I've needed to creatively avoid some topics and tell little white lies several times to keep my secret. I didn't see him this past winter—it's not a lie, but it is a lie by omission. I did spend the night with him last June before he left for minor league baseball. We haven't been alone together since his last night in Athens, but I do share a daughter with Hamilton. Here goes another avoidance of the truth that I hope they don't hate me for in the years to come.

"We did not have a secret rendezvous during the off-season. I must confess I was caught off-guard by his actions last night, too." I nervously shrug. "I've got a tropical storm swirling inside my head. I'm mega confused." I swirl my index finger in a circle above my head.

"Did he call you today?" Salem asks.

I answer that he probably spent the day trying to catch up with the team on the East Coast while catching up on his sleep for tomorrow's game where he takes the mound, they attempt to make me feel better by stating they are sure he will call tomorrow.

"What should I do when he calls?" I know they don't know the major details that led up to last night, but I still need some advice.

Bethany tells me to play it cool and let him explain when he is ready. Salem seems stumped and Savannah says I should demand answers. So, no help from these three. Adrian might be better help, but she would also poke and pry until I cracked revealing our night together last June and that we have a daughter. She'd see right through my lie that I have no idea what might have prompted his actions.

Lucky for me, Bethany states she really must get back to Troy and their baby-making. I'm made to promise I will keep them posted on Hamilton's explanations when we do finally talk before we end this week's call.

The weight of the secrets I am keeping from Hamilton, his family, and my friends grows heavier tonight. Part of me wonders if Hamilton is settled enough in his career that revealing we have a daughter might not lead him to leave the Cubs and move back to Athens. But another stronger part of me wants to give him until the end of this season. Not wanting to wallow any longer, I decide to slip on my flip-flops and join Alma, Liberty, and McGee on the rest of their walk.

4

HAMILTON

Not even the cold post-practice ice strapped to my left shoulder and elbow can pull my thoughts from Madison. My bullpen catcher and pitching coach reprimanded me for not keeping my head on my job today.

Although she's filled most of my thoughts over the past year, everything changed yesterday. A switch flipped inside of me, I can't fight my feelings and now I can't get Madison off my mind.

The moment I walked out from changing into my wedding attire to match the guys, I felt my world shift. All of the air in the barn left—I felt like I took a punch to the gut. I couldn't breathe. Madison stood hands on hips in cowboy boots, a tutu, and denim vest. Although she dressed just as all of Adrian's friends for the ceremony, on her it worked. My tumultuous thoughts clicked into place like a puzzle piece. My body hummed to life in a way that did not say she was my best friend. It became clear that I wanted more than friendship—I wanted *every* part of her. I needed Madison.

In the hours that followed I found myself constantly touching her —she called to me. I played with her hair and leaned closer than usual to whisper in her ear as I reveled in her scent. My lips found their way to her cheeks and temples many times during the evening, but I longed for more.

The favor she asked of me my last night in Athens plunged her into the starring role of every one of my fantasies. That one night with Madison has played on my spank bank reel ever since.

Yeah, I know it sounds bad. I had a one-night-stand with my virginal best friend on my last night in town. Instead of putting myself on the market in Des Moines and Chicago, I relive that night while in the shower and in my bed. I sound like a creep.

She almost slipped away last night. At the stop sign where we would drive in opposite directions, I had to make my move. I darted from my car to hers. When she lowered her window, my brain failed me, and my heart took over. I leaned in, covered her lips with mine, and poured all of my feelings into our kiss. Madison's lips shared the feelings she'd been hiding from me, too. When I pulled back to catch my breath, her wide eyes, flushed face, and swollen lips parted as they gasped for breath. The vision is now burned in my mind. She wanted me, and my kiss affected her.

Luckily, my brain kicked in and knew I needed to drive, or I'd miss my flight and today's practice. My parting words haunt me, 'Eleven months seemed like an eternity away from you. Drive careful. I love you.' After my confession, I jogged to my car and drove away from my best friend, the girl who owns my heart.

I wince as I adjust the icepack on my shoulder. I attempted to share my true feelings for her during every phone conversation for eleven months. Many times, I opened my mouth, the words on the tip of my tongue, then froze. I promised her our one night together, her 'virginity favor' wouldn't change our friendship. I really did try for months to erase that one night from my mind to allow me to just be friends again. But during our phone calls, I felt her through the receiver. She shared her new college-life, her hectic schedule, about her new friend Alma, and her fears. With each conversation, my heart grew, and I fell deeper in love with my best friend Madison.

Last night I shared my feelings—I admitted I love her. Of course, I quickly ran to my car to hide as soon as I spoke the words, but I meant them. I hope she knows how much I meant my kiss and words. I hope she wants me like I want her. I need her to love me and not just as best friends love each other.

Coach's gruff voice cuts into my silent reflections. "Armstrong, we need your mind on throwing and not back in Podunk Missouri. Don't make me regret letting you take an unscheduled day off. Lock. It. Down." Watching the coach's back as he walks from the training room, I vow to keep my thoughts on baseball when at work and save my confusing thoughts of Madison for my private time.

5

MADISON

As May fades into June, my texts and calls with Hamilton remain as they were prior to Adrian's wedding. I don't allude to our good bye. I allow him time to focus on his pitching and to work out his feelings. I'm sure he is as confused as I am.

This week I began my senior year of college by taking summer classes. My goal to fast track my education came to fruition. I begin student teaching this fall, have my college graduation in December, and hopefully I will secure a teaching position for the spring semester. My summer classes move at a rapid pace providing me with many hours of homework each day. So, this morning Liberty is enjoying tummy time on her quilt in the center of the floor while I finish up my lesson plan assignment for Monday's class.

I find my eyes constantly drift to my daughter when I should be working. She's currently holding her head up and babbling at her nearby toys. I slide my laptop to the side of the sofa and crawl down to join her. We babble, she drools, and we smile. She's growing too fast. Everyday there is something new—Hamilton is missing too much. My ringing phone interrupts our playtime.

"I love you baby girl," I whisper to my sleepy daughter. "One day, you will meet your daddy. You will meet Bethany and Troy, Adrian and Winston, Salem and Latham, and my friend Savannah." I kiss her cheek. "For now, it's time for a bottle and little girls to nap."

6

HAMILTON

Sitting on the air-conditioned charter bus waiting for my teammates to arrive, I turn my iPhone to entertain myself. The post-game interviews and showers droned on today. I'm irritable. Our long road trip is taking its toll on me.

Finally, the bus pulls from the stadium, escorting us back to our nearby Minneapolis hotel. My life is a blur of hotels, shuttles, airplanes, and restaurant food. While I enjoy every minute at our country's ballparks, the rest of the traveling is torture. My life depends upon my teammates to pack, load, and unload the airplanes and shuttle busses. A handful of players are perpetually late, slower than the rest, and inconsiderate of everyone's time.

It's nearly 7:00 p.m., we're hungry, we're tired, we're sore, and we need time away from each other. We're not even halfway through our 162-game season. We are on our final leg of a fourteen-game road trip, and most of us need time away from the other twenty-four men in the traveling circus that is our Chicago Cubs team.

As a boy dreaming of playing Major League Baseball, I looked forward to traveling. Now, I detest away games and all that they entail. I crave a home-cooked meal. Phone conversations with Madison and my mom stir my homesick feelings even more. I miss my mom and the farm, I miss hanging with Madison, and I'm tired of eating alone.

We won today's game after eleven innings, thus we're later than usual, returning to the hotel. As I take the mound tomorrow, I'll stay in this evening. I have a pregame meal and routine I never stray from. I'll have chicken breast and steamed vegetables delivered to my room. I'll study my opponents for tomorrow's game, then shoot a text to Madison before I turn in for the night. I never imagined how lonely and exhausting being a professional ball player could be.

7

MADISON

I've asked Alma to care for Liberty while I drive to Athens and back today. My heartaches at the thought of time away from my baby, but I've never missed a Father's Day with my dad. Although this year it requires careful planning, I find a way to make it possible. I've reached out to Hamilton's mother, Memphis, asking if I might drop by her place this morning and enjoy lunch with her. Of course, she is thrilled with the promise of my long overdue visit. The Cubs play today, so I will not run into Hamilton during this visit to our hometown—a fact that is both a relief and a disappointment.

It's days like this when the double-life I lead haunts me. I need to talk to Hamilton. My world is over-complicated. Talking to him will allow my two worlds to combine. I'll no longer hide my daughter while visiting Athens. I'll no longer dread such trips. Alma and Liberty would be able to travel with me. My three-hour drive wouldn't be as lonely. As this weekend drew closer, I debated my need to visit my father and I pondered remaining in Columbia this year.

I arrive at The Armstrong Farm just before ten to find Memphis chatting with three farm-hands as they sit on a truck tailgate near the barn. I make my way to her before she can end their conversation. I squeeze her from the side unable to restrain myself—visiting her excites me. Memphis introduces me to the men that help her keep the farm running. In our many phone conversations she's shared that many boys and men from surrounding farms and the Athens community offer to help her with crops, harvests, and livestock year-round.

I marvel at her fortitude in running this large farm without her husband and son. She's one of the two very strong women as mentors I'm blessed with in my life and I hope to be this strong in the eyes of my daughter.

Memphis wraps her arm around my shoulders as she escorts me toward the house. Everything seems just as it was last summer. Hamilton had just left for Des Moines to play minor league baseball and I spent much of my time with his mother. With iced tea in hand we take a seat in the shade on her porch swing.

She asks questions about my summer classes and placement for student teaching this fall. We discuss Hamilton and the exciting season the Cubs are having. I teasingly remind her I am a Cardinals fan, so we need to end our affections for the Cubs right there. Memphis fills me in on her daughter, the crops she has in, the new calves, and how much Troy has been assisting her.

As our conversation wanes a bit, thoughts of my gigantic secret creep into my mind. It would be easy to share my burden with her at this moment. I'd first explain my reason for not visiting last winter was due to my pregnancy. I could tell her I had a daughter on March 10th and explain it was a one-night stand. I know she would discuss my situation in great detail and support me from today on. She'd visit Columbia and insist I visit her more often with my daughter. It would feel so good to have her support.

But I can't tell her the father is her son—I can't ask her to keep my secret from her son. Upon laying eyes on Liberty, Memphis would instantly know Hamilton is her father. I've marveled at the many photos Memphis decorates her home with—Liberty is the spitting image of Hamilton's big sister. Earlier while Memphis excused herself to the bathroom and I poured our tea, I held a pic of Liberty on my phone next to a photo of Hamilton's sister at approximately the same age. Her brown curls, chocolate eyes, long lashes, even her Cupid's Bow lips are a mirror image of her aunt. Thus, there is no way I can confide in Memphis until I reveal to Hamilton. I don't regret my night with him or my daughter—I do regret keeping my secret. For now, this must be my burden and my burden alone. I clear my thoughts and return to my conversation with Memphis.

We snap a selfie on the porch swing and I Snapchat to Hamilton. We know he has an afternoon game today, so we don't expect him to reply. I've missed this. I spent much of my high school life with Hamilton and his mother, being near Memphis today demonstrates how much she means to me. While in Columbia, Alma fills the void formerly owned by Memphis. Alma's not her replacement, just another strong woman to guide me in the absence of my own mother.

From time-to-time I still dream my mother is in recovery, that slowly we mend fences, and I eventually share Liberty with her. I don't delude myself—it is only a silly dream. Liberty *will not* be exposed to her alcoholism. I want her nowhere near the constant hurt my mother inflicts on those around her. Alma fills the role of grandmother until I tell Hamilton and Memphis. Then, Liberty's family will grow in people and in love.

Out of the blue, Memphis asks me if Hamilton shares his personal life with me in texts or calls. My face scrunches not sure what she means. She explains he doesn't speak of dating or girls in any of his visits or calls to her. I let her know he claims girls mess with his game as I speak of blonde arm-candy or his dating.

"I'm not old-fashioned," Memphis begins. "I know he's no angel. I just hope he remembers our talks from high school about preventing pregnancy scares."

She searches my face for any knowledge I might have on her son's dating. I hope the fact he has a daughter with me doesn't show on my face. I try not to look guilty. I can't let her know that although we used condoms, I still became pregnant. I explain to Memphis that although I bring it up and tease him about women, he emphatically denies spending time with anyone.

She turns the tables to ask if I have dated in Columbia. I explain I am far too busy to waste time anywhere that men hang out. I confess a guy from Bible study asked me out and I opted instead for a group of us going out. I am focusing on me and my education right now—I don't need a boyfriend to add to my busy schedule. She encourages me to put myself out there to start the hunt for my future boyfriend.

I pretend to go along with it. I'm a single mom on a fast track to graduation, I have no time to spare. I don't share that anytime I'm not studying or sitting in class I'm focusing on Liberty. I sense Memphis has something she wants to ask me. Can she tell I'm keeping a secret? Although I wait she keeps it to herself.

8

MADISON

I say my goodbye to Memphis after lunch. The reason for this trip is to visit my dad and it's time that I head that way. During the ten-minute drive from the Armstrong farm to the cemetery, I contemplate how far I live now from my dad and how visiting once a year is not enough.

"Hey dad," I say out loud. "I'm here like I promised." I kneel next to his headstone. I brush the grass shavings and dust from the top and the engraved lettering of his light-gray granite stone. My mind floods with all I need to say. I wonder with him in heaven does he already know everything that happened to me in the last twelve months. "I love you." My words fail to tell him how much I miss and need him. I continue as if he isn't on my shoulder each and every day. I talk of Hamilton and Liberty, my classes, and Alma. I express my constant worry about my mother and how far she fell without him around. I share my plans for the upcoming year for my career, for Liberty, and for Hamilton. After several quiet moments, I promise I'll bring Liberty with me next time and say goodbye.

My phone buzzes as I walk from his headstone to my car at the edge of the cemetery.

Mother: I hope you miss your father today as much as I do

I freeze at her texted words. Is she guilting me? Is she sober enough to remember I visit his grave every year on Father's Day? She was rarely sober when I lived at home, so I doubt she is ever sober now that I am gone.

Me: I visit his grave EVERY Father's Day
Me: Hope you find 1 hour a year to visit him
Me: without alcohol in your system
Mother: year at college didn't soften your heart
Me: I've texted you & left voicemail for you every week for 52 weeks
Me: Not a word from you
Me: Until you are sober DON'T text me
Mother: after everything I have done for you
Me: I hope you are referring to the time before dad's death
Me: because the last 6 years I've been without a dad & a mom

I set my phone on Do Not Disturb mode. Now I can ignore her texts. I'm fuming—she has some nerve. The fact that she texted me at all shocks me. I assume she has at least half a bottle in her by now at home since the bars can't open on Sunday in Athens. For that matter, I'm surprised she even knows it is Father's Day.

I want to text her that she has a granddaughter and if she sobers up she can visit me, or I will visit her, but I've not the energy to hope anymore. I've been burned too many times. In the past I hoped, and I prayed, then I waited for her to be the mom I needed. She's perpetually on my prayer list. I've shared information and resources to help yet it is always me without her.

In my virtual Al-anon and Alateen meetings, I've learned I can't help her until she is ready to accept help. I've learned her actions don't reflect upon me and others don't hold me accountable for her actions. I've met so many others online in my same situation. We share our stories, our hopes, our prayers, and our reality that our own life is all that we may control.

With my phone no longer alerting me to her texts or calls, I sit in my car for a moment. I don't want to leave this way. I can't allow her to taint this visit, so I return to my dad's grave. Sitting in the green grass, I rest my right hand on his name.

"Dad, I miss you. I wish you were here. I know it's not your fault mother has fallen so far, but if you were here she might still be the mom I need. I have so many things in my life that I wish you were here to help me with. Liberty grows so fast. I know you would spoil her rotten. She would love visits to papa's farm—you would have a little helper at the hog lot and on your tractors." I wipe my tears from my chin. "She'd wrap you around her little finger."

I continue to wipe tears from my cheeks as I sit quietly for several long minutes. When my phone rings interrupting the silence, I realize it's one of the ten people I have on my favorites list, otherwise it wouldn't ring while on Do Not Disturb mode. A sad smile slides on my face when I see Hamilton's name and picture for this FaceTime call.

"Hello."

"Are you still in..." his words trail off. "Hey."

"Hey."

"Visiting your dad, I wish I was there with you right now." I'm not sure if it is the tears and my red puffy eyes, or the cemetery in the background that tipped him off. "We have a rain out and I was attempting to call you before you left Athens."

"Sorry about your game and yes you caught me just in time." I wipe my face on my sleeve trying to look less pathetic. "Did you need something?"

Hamilton's face falls a bit. "I thought if I caught you, I could ask you to do a favor for me."

"I can try." I begin walking back towards my car as we chat.

"Do you need to hurry back to Columbia?"

"Nope. Come on, it's me, just tell me what you need already." The more he avoids asking the favor, the more worried I become. Thoughts of him coming to Athens to see me, asking me to come to Chicago to visit him, plus many others swirl in my mind.

"Could you walk me over to my dad's headstone? I'd like to spend a moment with him for Father's Day, too."

I freeze. It's at this moment that I realize this is actually Hamilton's first Father's Day and he doesn't even know it. Liberty should be spending the day with her daddy. We could have bought him a gift or two and a sweet card. My heart weighs a ton in my chest. This is yet another milestone I deprive them of.

"Mady..." Hamilton's voice draws me back.

"Yeah, sure, no problem." I change my direction walking towards Mr. Armstrong's final resting place on the opposite end of the cemetery from my dad's. "I'm glad you called when you did. A few more minutes and I would have already been speeding down the highway."

At the graveside, I turn the camera view from me to the headstone. I remove my shoes and prop my cell phone between them angled up with a full view of his father's stone. I peek into the camera's line of sight. "I propped the camera up. I'll take a walk for a few minutes so the two of you can have some time alone. I'll announce myself when I walk back." I smile into the camera hoping Hamilton knows I'll still be with him in my thoughts as I take my walk.

"Thank you."

I look at my Fitbit on my wrist noting it is 2:15 p.m. I wander down and back through several rows of headstones. I recognize many common last names of Athens as I read each monument. I keep track of the birthdates trying to see what the oldest date I might find is. The stones here are not as old as the ones in the little cemetery near our farm that Hamilton and I spent many hours in during high school.

As I return to my phone fifteen minutes later, I announce here I come a few times as I approach. I'm caught off guard to find Hamilton is no longer connected. I wonder why he hung up or if he was disconnected. As I slip my shoes back on, I notice he texted me.

Hamilton: TY(thank you)
Hamilton: Call when you are on highway
Hamilton: I'll keep U company for part of drive
Me: Ok, call in about 10 min

Before leaving Athens, I stop for gas and a few snacks then pull onto the highway pointed back towards Liberty, Alma, and my other life in Columbia.

"Libby," Alma plays. "Look at my tractor." Alma pushes the large toy with soft edges, resembling a tractor forward on the blanket.

My mind drifts to my times helping my dad on the farm. Liberty would enjoy riding on my dad's lap as he drove the tractors. I envision her sitting alone in the seat while he climbed down to open the gates to the pasture. Dad would help her ride a goat and I'm sure he would buy her a pony when she was old enough. My mind easily flips through the many farm activities my dad would enjoy sharing with his granddaughter.

I fight back my tears at the interactions Liberty will never have with my dad. Come to think of it, Libby will never have a grandfather as Hamilton's father also passed away. I lost all four of my grandparents before I turned five. With the current situation with my mother, Alma and someday soon Memphis will be the only grandparents she will know.

Of course, now thoughts of my mother are all I can think of. Although I think of her from time-to-time, I don't worry about her every day. I love my new life free of a daily reminder of the danger my mother carries with her. I have a routine. It's smooth. I do not miss the perpetual out-of-control feeling I once carried around while living with my alcoholic mother. I've resigned to the fact she is who she is and lives the life she chooses. I have removed myself, moved on as best I can, and have Troy to inform me when anything goes wrong. It's all I can handle and enjoy my life as I deserve to.

9

HAMILTON

The tiny red two alerts me I have Snapchats to view. As is my habit, I quickly snap a screenshot of each allowing me more time to view them. The first pic is a selfie of Madison on the porch swing with my mother. They are the two most important people in my life and it warms my heart they still get together in my absence. I trace my finger over Madison's giant smile. Her golden-tanned face glows and bright blue eyes twinkle in the summer sun. She's happy—they both seem happy. It reads 'wish you were here'. The second picture displays a view of the barn from the driver's seat of the tractor. Madison typed 'Must feed the cows'. If only they knew how I longed for my former farm life.

Although Madison stated she'd go for a walk and alert me of her return, I hope she will stand nearby and listen.

"I love you, dad and I'm sorry I can't be there in person." I clear my throat, my mouth suddenly very dry. "I'm still in Minneapolis. They called the game after five innings and an hour of rain and lightning delay. I'm still living our dream and feel your presence every time I take the mound." A chuckle escapes as I prepare to share about the game. "I took a chance in the third inning. The guys shared that the coach's face turned beet-red and he cursed twice before he changed to cheering for me. It kills me to bunt at each of my at-bats. I decided today to the show coach what I've been telling him all season. The count was 2-0. Ever cocky Mosby gift-wrapped a fastball right down the middle. I wish you could have seen his face when I took a full swing knocking his gift in the upper section of the left-center bleachers. I was just so tired of American League pitchers assumed to be an easy out via bunt. I now have one homerun and two RBI's on my stats. In a long conversation with the manager and batting coach, they've decided to let me officially bat instead of bunt for the rest of the season."

I run my fingers through my hair. "They'll soon be knocking on my hotel room door signaling it's time to head to the airport." I sigh as I organize all I wish to share with dad today.

"I'm in love with Madison." I blurt then quietly listen to see if I hear a reaction from Madison if she remained within earshot. Hearing nothing, I continue. "It kills me to be in Chicago with her in Columbia. I long to share my life with her. It's lonely in my condo and on the road as much as the Cubs are. I try to share everything with her via our texts and calls. Hearing her voice helps some. I miss her every day. I need her more now than ever before, both mentally and physically." Again, I chuckle. "I showed her and told her I loved her at the end of May. Then we each returned to our lives."

"Dad, I'm lost and need you now more than ever. How do I allow her to chase her dream while I chase mine, yet show her how much I love her? I need you to guide me. I need you to help me. She's too close to mom. If I ask for mom's help, you know her, she would get her hopes up. If something were to happen and we don't become a couple both Madison and mom would be devastated. I can't risk their friendship with each other until I figure out how to make us work. You know what I mean? I'm sure you do. I need one of your deep philosophical conversations we shared while mending fences or sitting at the livestock barn. I desperately need your guidance. So, I'll be looking for your signs. Just remember I'm a novice at love and might need more than a gentle prod in the right direction."

Knock. Knock. Knock.

"Well, I've gotta go. I love and miss you so much, dad. I hope I make you proud."

10

MADISON

As the heat of July in the Midwest takes a firm grip on the exposed throat of the Midwest, Alma and I begin walking Liberty and McGee early in the morning or after seven in the evening. My summer classes require me to leave late morning and return mid-afternoon when the sun is the hottest. I'm thankful my old car's air conditioner still works.

The three of us take a mini-weekend-vacation to St. Louis. It will be a weekend of firsts for Liberty. I'm excited to share my love for the St. Louis Cardinals while she sees her daddy pitch for the first time. We plan to attend the Saturday evening and Sunday afternoon games. We settle into our hotel room to relax a bit after our long drive. Liberty slept as I drove. Now she is awake and hungry. Alma offers to feed her while I unpack then set up the portable crib.

Due to the heat, we arrive only thirty minutes before the first pitch. Alma assists as I record Liberty with eyes open entering the ballpark and in our lower level seats for the video journal I keep to share with Hamilton in the future. I smile to myself as she and I wear our Cardinals jerseys. Libby has a red headband in her dark brown curls. By the first pitch, her yawns grow more frequent. Alma pulls a bottle from the diaper bag. Liberty's eyes lock on it immediately while her legs and arms begin to animate with excitement.

Fans sitting in the seats around us laugh at her reaction. One kind Cardinals fan offers to take a picture of the three of us with the field in the background while her husband holds the baby bottle. She claims we need a photo while Libby is awake of all of us at her first game. Fortunately, Libby cooperates. I'm surprised she didn't start to cry as her bottle moved farther away instead of closer. When my little girl is hungry she doesn't like to wait for her food.

When her tummy is full she falls sound asleep. I place her in the baby sling swaddled to my chest for the remainder of the game. Alma snaps photos occasionally of Libby and I, the game, and beautiful Busch Stadium all lit up after dark. Between the fifth and sixth inning a camera zooms in on the sleeping Libby still wearing her red Cardinals headband and me. We are projected on the jumbotron. A loud 'ahh' erupts from the stadium. Luckily a fan nearby snaps a picture of us on the big screen and asks to text it to me.

I stare at the perfect photo on my phone screen for many minutes. Suddenly fear envelops me. What if Hamilton heard the 'ah' and glanced at the jumbotron? He would no doubt recognize me. He might have seen Liberty. My heartbeat quickens. Please, please, please don't let him have seen us.

"Madison," Alma's concerned voice calls. "What's wrong?" She places her hand on my forearm.

I quietly share my concern that Hamilton might have seen me on the jumbotron with Liberty. Alma calmly asks to see the photo on my phone. She studies it for a moment. She points out with my Cardinals hat and Libby at my chest, Hamilton might simply think it was someone that resembles me. Most of my face is shaded by the hat, Alma isn't in the shot, and he has no reason to think I would bring a baby girl to a ballgame. Her words calm most of my fears. I'll need to wait until I hear from him next to see if he brings it up to know for sure.

The next day, Libby wakes from her nap as we enter the stadium. I selected seats in the shade for this sultry day to ensure she remains as cool as possible. Alma records me helping Libby clap when her daddy is announced as the starting pitcher for the Chicago Cubs. Today, I wear my Cardinals attire while Libby wears her daddy's jersey, a Cubs diaper cover, and a blue Cubs headband in her damp ringlets. Alma and I keep our voices low when we refer to Hamilton as Libby's daddy. We don't want anyone to hear us and start rumors on social media about Hamilton having a daughter. I am acutely aware he is in the public eye.

Hamilton's pitches vex my Cardinals. The Cards trail by two when he leaves the game in the seventh. Alma and I decide due to the heat we should leave, too. At Alma's van, we remove the plastic bags she insisted we keep in the cooler. In each of the three bags Alma placed a washcloth for after the game. Yet another trick I've learned in our time together. I wipe Liberty down from head to toe, change her diaper, then secure her in her car seat for the drive home. Alma and I use our washcloths on the back of our neck and face to cool down as I drive.

11

HAMILTON

It's one-hundred five degrees on the turf at game time. With the hot July sun bearing down and all eyes on me, I deliver the first pitch in the bottom of the first inning. It's a ninety-eight-mph fastball for a strike. Cardinal fans boo loudly from all directions as I play with the rosin bag in my left hand. A smirk graces my face as I realize Madison both cheers for me and groans for her team. I mentally chide myself. Not at work. I must not let thoughts of Madison affect my work. With my head back in the game and a strike under my belt the oppressive heat melts away and I find my rhythm.

During the top of the third inning I mentally prepare myself to face the bottom of the St. Louis line-up as well as hit this inning. As I stand at the edge of the dugout I pray Stan gets on, so I can bat this inning.

While securing my batting gloves, Humphreys leans close. "Your girl's a huge Cardinal's fan, isn't she?" He chuckles while his elbow prods my ribcage. "Don't hold anything back to make her happy. Our team comes first."

Is this guy for real? Have my six strikeouts and one walk not demonstrated my loyalty to the Cubs? I try to remind myself Humphreys is angry I get to hit as a pitcher. My homerun and RBI total are quickly approaching his stats. It wouldn't look good for a pitcher to put up better stats than a fielder with many more at bats. I smile knowing Madison wants me to succeed, even against her Cardinals. I wish she were in the stands today as I approach the batter's box.

With a 2-1 count, I connect with the next pitch and send it soaring over the centerfield wall. I begin my homerun trot amidst St. Louis boos and knowledge my homerun and 2 RBI's pissed Humphreys off even more.

The pitching coach pulls me from the mound in the bottom of the seventh inning. The Cubs lead six to three, I leave with a double, a homerun, and three RBI's along with my many strikeouts from the mound. Although I struggled keeping my fingertips dry in the sweltering July heat, I had a great showing today.

As I sit, icing my shoulder and elbow on the bench. I lose my battle to keep my thoughts off Madison at work. I look forward to chatting with her tonight. I wanted to arrange a visit with her while I was in St. Louis, but this long road trip kept me too busy. With the All-Star break later this month, perhaps I can arrange some time for the two of us. I mentally flip through my upcoming schedule. Home games this week for the Fourth of July, photo shoot and endorsement meetings between games, and three days off for the All-Star break on the Fifteenth. Not much time to work with. I'll need to confirm a few things tomorrow, then I can schedule time with Madison during the three-day break.

I long for the day we live in the same city, are a real couple, and we can relive the entire game together as we did in high school. I dream of a relationship with Madison more with each passing week. In the upcoming off-season I plan to move us forward—I plan to make her mine.

12

MADISON

My phone signals a text from Adrian shortly after we leave St. Louis. Alma reads each text while I remain focused on the road.

Adrian: Can't call tonight
Adrian: Dinner with Winston's parents
Adrian: Sorry

I ask Alma to text her back for me.

Me: I understand
Adrian: Twice as much gossip for next Sunday
Me: (smile emoji)

I'm surprised that I'm not more upset by her texts. Over the past year, we've only missed three Sunday evening calls. Lately, each call leaves me sad. I'm no longer a constant in the lives of my friends. Perhaps the decision to keep my daughter a secret pulls me farther from my friends.

I fill the kitchen sink with warm water, gather bath items from the nursery, then announce to Liberty it's time for a bath. She loves the water as much as I enjoy watching her in it.

Barely sitting in the sink, Liberty begins slapping her palms against the water while cheering and spraying me with warm droplets. As I pretend to protest, she laughs her adorable deep-belly laugh. Alma joins our fun time.

When my cell vibrates on the counter, Alma offers to play with Liberty while I check it.

Hamilton: Busy?
Me: Never too busy for u

Immediately my cell phone signals and incoming FaceTime call. I step from the kitchen after Alma takes over bath duty, briskly seeking my quiet bedroom as I answer.

"Is it raining there?" Hamilton's voice greets.

"No, why?"

His laughter causes my belly to flip-flop. Liberty laughs just like her daddy. I quickly lie claiming I was cleaning my shower.

I take in his dress clothes and use of his Bluetooth ear piece. He's not on an airplane. "Where are you?"

Hamilton explains he's on the shuttle from O'Hare back to Wrigley. "I wanted to call you before it got too late." His hushed tone calls to every cell in me. I recall this whispered voice while cuddling in his arms, his lips near my ear.

"Madison," he calls to me. "Where'd you go just now?" His chocolate eyes squint as his brow furrows.

I shake it off. "You had a great game today." I mentally scold myself for my lustful thoughts as I change the subject.

"Tell me you didn't hear your Cardinal fans boo me through your TV."

"Actually, Alma and I were at the game today." I witness shock slide over his face. "I cheered for you on the inside while Alma jumped up and down in her Armstrong jersey beside me."

"Crap!" Hamilton turns to his right informing his teammate everything is okay. Looking back into his phone, he rejoins our call. "I wanted to plan dinner or something while in St. Louis. I got so busy with the long road trip that I couldn't get the logistics straightened out." He runs his hands from his scalp slowly down his face. This draws my attention to his dark brown tired eyes. "I can't believe you were in Busch Stadium today and I didn't get to see you. You were so close..."

"With my summer classes and your schedule, I'm not sure it would've worked out." I can't take the sad eyes he now stares back at me with. "Alma and I had to make a quick day trip to squeeze the game in. We left when they made the pitching change."

"I need to check on a few things tomorrow." A small smile slips upon his perfect lips. "What does your schedule look like from the 15th though the 17th?"

My eyes look to the ceiling as I attempt to recall my calendar. "That's dead week. I'll have projects to work on, papers to write, and finals to study for." His smile fades and the twinkle in his eye disappears. "But, I can shift things to squeeze you in."

"That's my number one fan," he teases. "Give me a day or two then we'll make our plans."

"I hate to seem like I don't want to see you, but what happens when you make the All-Star roster?" I *know* Hamilton doesn't believe he stands a chance his first full season with the Cubs, but I know he will be playing in this season's All-Star Game. Which means he will be much too busy to visit me. As much as I want to see him, it's easier than arranging a visit and asking Alma to keep Liberty for me.

Hamilton rises from his charter-bus seat, he promises to call me in a day or two, then ends our call with an 'I love you'. His teammates within earshot catcall and tease him as he disconnects.

My mind reels. Hamilton stated he loves me in earshot of his team. He pretty much just outed our long-distance relationship to his closest friends. Relationship. Is it really a relationship? We haven't been on a first date. We only share conversations via text and phone calls a couple of times a week. He did step things up a notch at Adrian's wedding over a month ago, but he hasn't really made it clear where we stand since then.

The remainder of the night I spend reliving every word, touch, and kiss from May until now. Even though I give up finding there's no way I can figure out what's in his head, sleep evades me for many hours.

13

MADISON

Mid-week I receive a call from Adrian as I am driving to my class. "Hi," I answer leery why she calls at a time she knows I am headed to class for the day.

"Can you talk for a couple of minutes?" she asks instead of a greeting. When I let her know I have ten minutes before class begins she continues. "Bethany lost the baby early this morning. We are just leaving the hospital to get her settled back at home."

Bile rises up my throat as my stomach burns. I have no words for this news. My heart aches for my dear friend.

"I know." Adrian assures me—she understands my current inability to process this horrible news. "Call me this afternoon. I will give you more details and let you know how she is doing at home. I'm sorry I dropped this on you before class, but I couldn't slip away earlier at the hospital and couldn't wait until three this afternoon to tell you. I didn't want someone to text you about it, and you not know what they were referring to."

"Thank you." My voice is hoarse,

"Try to focus during class. I realize it will be hard, but there is nothing anyone can do but pray for Bethany and Troy." Adrian's attempts do nothing to comfort me as we disconnect.

Walking into the classroom, I turn on the voice recorder app in my phone to keep track of items covered today. When I walk out hours later, I can't recall a thing the professor covered. I'm glad I thought to use the recorder—my mind was on Bethany, how much she longed for a family, the miscarriage, and Troy. Even now as I unlock my car I fight tears. I crave Alma's help processing Bethany's tragedy.

When I arrive home, Alma attempts to comfort me as she shares a wealth of information. She admits she had two miscarriages—one before her oldest child was born and one before her second child. She explains that is how she met Dr. Anderson the first time. Of course, he was much younger back then than last March when he delivered Liberty for me. Alma shares both of her experiences in great detail.

After dinner, with tissues in hand for my leaking eyes, I continue my online research. I visit health sites covering the clinical side of miscarriages and recovery. I find several sites focused on successfully conceiving that explain the causes and likelihood of miscarriages. Then they positively paint the months following a miscarriage and steps toward conceiving again.

Having struggled with my own bouts of depression, I understand the loneliness, despair, and the feeling of being lost lying ahead of Bethany and Troy. Although I will continue to hope the couple successfully mourns, heals, and tries again—I know they will struggle. It's hard to accept help and open up to others when one falls into the dark pit. It's a journey comparable to climbing up Mt. Everest to find your way back out.

I startle when Alma slaps my laptop closed. I look up through my wet lashes at her expressionless face.

"That's enough. There are too many horror stories on the web and no amount of research will help Bethany." She forces a smile. "Be there when she calls. Be the daily phone call that makes her day. Listen when she needs an ear. That's all you can do for her." Alma wraps her arms around me from behind while I remain seated. I absorb her words and her warmth.

Liberty doesn't enjoy floor time this evening. I keep my daughter on my lap in my arms. I've always believed her to be my little miracle —now I better understand the blessing I have with my healthy daughter.

I memorize once more every little finger, toe, and dimple. I marvel at her dark curly hair like Hamilton's. I take in the changes of the four months since I first held her in my arms at the hospital.

With Liberty tucked in for the night, I turn in early. I continue to struggle. Athens feels like it's on the other side of the planet from me. Three hours is too far to drive with my schedule to spend some time with Bethany. I feel the deep need to be with her, to help her, and to hug her tightly as she cries. My friend is hurting—my phone calls don't seem enough. Bethany and Troy's large families and their Athens friends will surround them. I have no doubt she will be well taken care of—I wish I could be there, too.

The next day, Bethany calls me at 5:00 p.m. I excuse myself to my room silently pointing to ask Alma to watch Libby while she grabs the toys on her blanket. I say a quick prayer to be strong enough to carry on a conversation with Bethany without too much crying. She needs me to listen and comfort her, not to cry like a baby.

"Hey honey."

"Madison," Bethany's quivering voice weakly whispers. "Is this a good time?"

I assure her I am here anytime she wants to call and chat. I ask how she is today because I know *how she is doing*. My friend will not be good for quite a while. She shares the entire heartbreaking story. She woke up around 2:00 a.m. spotting on her sheets. Having read that can sometimes happen she wasn't worried until she went to the restroom where cramping and a gush of bright red blood occurred. She screamed to wake up Troy and they hurried to the emergency room. She claims Troy remained calm and tried to calm her as well. It seems he was strong in this situation just as my friend needed.

As she shares the rest of the story, my heart breaks for her all over again.

Silently I think maybe it's a good thing I've kept my secret. It might be hard for Bethany to talk to me if she knew I am already a mother she desires to be. With her fluctuating hormones and recent loss, I might more like an enemy than a friend. I focus on Bethany once again.

"Adrian spent the morning with me, today then Salem came for the afternoon. She left minutes ago as Troy should be home anytime now." Bethany's words cause red flags to pop up.

"Did he go to work today?" It's a stupid question—she just alluded to him being gone all day. I cannot believe he didn't stay home at least one day with her. She wanted a baby and to start their family—it's all she could talk about. She needs him today. They lost a baby, both of them need to grieve and comfort each other. "Bethany, if you need him to stay with you, you may have to tell him. I'm sure he will stay if he knows you need him."

"He spent yesterday afternoon and evening with me. Once he tucked me into bed, he slept on the sofa. I didn't even hear him get ready this morning before he left." A tearful hiccup escapes. Bethany attempts to gather herself to continue. "I'm sure he thought I would just sleep all day today."

"Did you want him to stay with you today?" My voice is gruffer than it should be. Bethany needs my support not my anger.

"Yeah, I think so. I mean it never occurred to me he might not be there when I woke up this morning. He did text me to tell me he arranged for Adrian to visit this morning."

"Bethany, promise me you will talk to him about this tonight. Just mention how sad you were that you didn't see him when you woke up. Tell him you missed him today. Honey, he's a guy—you have to spell it out for him. Okay?"

"Yeah." She pauses to blow her nose.

"So how are you physically? Any pain?"

"I'm just tired and still spotting a tiny bit." Bethany sighs deeply. "Now I have to wait six weeks to have a period and maybe a month or two after that before we may be able try again." Her sobs grow louder in my ear. I allow her several minutes to let it all out.

"Honey, you have to allow your body time to repair itself. I'm sure your doctor wants to make sure everything is okay before you get pregnant again. I know you want a baby right now, but even with waiting you could have a baby by this time next year." I hope my words provide comfort.

"When I got home from class yesterday, I shared your news with Alma. Honey, she had two miscarriages and has three healthy children. Taylor was born within a year of her first miscarriage. She wanted me to let you know she is here if you ever want to talk to her about it. She's helped me with so much already, so talking to her might be a good thing when you are ready. I'll text you her number later tonight, okay?"

I hope Bethany reaches out. Hearing from others might renew her hope of a family in the future, while also helping her cope with this painful loss.

"Troy's home."

"Bethany," I call, wanting to remind her one more time. "Please talk to Troy tonight. Tell him what you want, what you need from him, and how you feel. He's hurting, too. He may try to keep it all inside to protect you and that won't be a good thing. You need each other right now."

"I promise," her quiet voice answers. She quickly lets me go before Troy enters the house.

I worry for my friend. She's hurting, and Troy is avoiding her. Although she has a large family, lots of close friends, and is active in her church, I fear she may need a different kind of help in the upcoming months. I set a reminder in my calendar app every afternoon at four to check on Bethany. I'm aware there is only so much I can do from here, so I need to do what I can even if it's only a phone call to let her know I care.

Returning to the living room, I spot Alma holding on to Libby's hands as she toddles across the floor. Libby jabbers excitedly the entire way. When they turn my daughter's eyes and smile lighten my mood.

"Come here." I make 'gimme-gimme' gestures. "Come to mama. You can do it. Come on Libby." With Alma's support she tiptoes toward me.

Less than a step away, I scoop up my daughter placing a raspberry on her neck. Giggles erupt from my tiny human. I squeeze her tight against my chest needing her to comfort my worries for Bethany. Alma pats my shoulder as she heads to the kitchen for drinks.

14

MADISON

On the Eighth, I search Twitter a few times during class anxiously awaiting the release of the All-Star rosters. I know in my heart he'll make it—I just need official confirmation.

Finally, my phone vibrates in my pocket. I click the link in the tweet, scroll past the American League Roster for now, and there it is. He did it. His fans voted. Hamilton made the All-Star Team his first full season in the Majors.

I fidget in my chair. An hour of class remains. *How will I ever sit still?* After a couple more minutes, I gather my items and slip out the door. My mind is not on today's class—I decide it won't hurt anything for me to leave early.

On the way to my car, I don't notice the hot July sun as I shoot a text.

Me: Congrats!
Me: I told you. Why do you ever doubt me?

I excitedly drive home to celebrate with Liberty and Alma. Hamilton should already be at the ballpark for tonight's game as they host San Francisco. I will celebrate with them, until he calls me after the game and I can celebrate with him.

Hamilton: Don't gloat

I glance up from my laptop, noting it's nearly 11:00 pm. I clear my college work from my thoughts.

Me: How excited are you?

I don't wait for him to call me before I FaceTime him. He's standing outside his condo-elevator when he answers.

"If I lose you on the elevator, I'll call you right back." It's not the greeting I expect.

"Oh, sorry. I just wanted to see you. It's the next best thing to congratulating you in person."

"I'm glad you called. I needed to see you. Things never seem real until I can share them with you."

My heart melts with his words. He's in the elevator now and I'm thankful we didn't lose our connection.

"Can I entice you to spend a few days in Cincinnati with me?"

I bite my lower lip while gazing into his pleading puppy dog eyes. I'm going to make him sadder. A large hand squeezes tight around my heart. It always comes to this. Our schedules never quite sync up. It's a tiny part of the reason I keep putting off letting him meet Liberty.

"Hey," his voice attempts to soothe. "It's okay—I know you are busy that week." He runs his hand through his thick waves, now seated in his living room. His masculine tongue licks his lips before he continues. "It's been a long two months and I'm ready to see you in person. Don't get me wrong, I live for the chats and calls. It's just not the same. I long to hold you in my arms."

He's killing me. At the sight of his tongue, I fantasize it upon mine. My blood loudly pulses in my ears, my girly bits spark to attention, I wiggle in my bed praying he doesn't notice my need to rub my thighs together.

"Ham," my voice quivers divulging just how much his words have affected me. "I can't travel that week, I'll have too many things to complete for my classes. I'd love to experience your first All-Star Week..."

"I understand. My schedule is busier than yours. It's just frustrating."

15

HAMILTON

My schedule continues to prevent my spending time with Madison. My plans to make her mine can't happen if I can't be with her. I long to take her on our first date. I want to demonstrate how important she is to me in every way. I dream of holding her close in public to let the world know she's mine. While at dinner I want to show her off, then I plan to enjoy her privately at home.

While I've masturbated to the memory of our one night together more times than I care to admit, I need to reconnect with her intimately. I long to hear her pants, her moans, and the sound of my name on her lips when she finds her release. I hope our calls leave her as hot and bothered as I find myself. I've imagined her pleasuring herself in bed after we disconnect. Perhaps she relives our night together as I do—I'm sure it's not as often as I do though.

16

MADISON

Hamilton: Hopping on jet to Cincinnati
Me: Fly safe
Me: call if U get a chance
Hamilton: We're attending Homerun Derby
Hamilton: U should watch
Me: Always do
Hamilton: Gotta go

I read into each text. He's as excited as a little boy. It's got to be pretty exciting for him to watch his friends in the Homerun Derby then play in the All-Star Game. I wish I were there with him instead of working on my two papers tonight and studying tomorrow.

McGee whines tapping my arm with his paw as he lays on the floor alongside me. He's pouting that we won't let him into the backyard while it's raining. Poor puppy. It was too hot to walk earlier and now it's raining. I stop typing my paper to pet him. Alma invites him over to the sofa for loves—she claims I need to focus on my paper and not McGee. I'm almost done with my second draft of my second paper. She's right, if I focus I can take a break when the derby begins.

My fingertips continue to click clack away for twenty minutes more. I close my laptop with a flourish announcing I am done for the night. Alma carries in our snacks for the evening and we find a comfortable seat in time for the broadcast to begin.

The announcers welcome us to the All-Star festivities then introduce the finalists for tonight's competition. Liberty fusses loudly for a moment, then the sounds of her soiling her diaper fill the room. Leave it to my daughter to expertly choose a quiet transition to commercial to make such unladylike noises. McGee darts to the backdoor and Alma follows to let him out for only a minute. I wish I could run with them from the task at hand. I lay the changing mat on the carpet and proceed to change Liberty's diaper.

The announcers return as I place Liberty back on her blanket surrounded by her favorite toys. "This year's Homerun Derby holds two new twists. First, all pitches will be delivered at ninety-eight mph by a pitching machine. This has led to much discussion on social media leading up to tonight's broadcast. Second, starting off our first round and now standing at homeplate is our 'Mystery Contestant'.

"For our viewers at home, I would like to explain what we at the stadium witnessed during the commercial break. The large four-sided white screen contraption on wheels you now see around homeplate slowly rolled from the outfield bullpen, down the foul line to its current location. The entire time we observed the dark shadow of this 'Mystery Contestant' walking inside it. Notice how he stands swinging his bat at homeplate."

The second announcer continues, "Every precaution has been taken to conceal his true identity. Neither of us in the broadcast booth know his identity. No cameras are inside the four-sided contraption ensuring the crowd knows not who we have before us. They're telling us now only three camera angles will be available to record his homerun attempts. There will be no camera angles from the field toward homeplate."

The other announcer jumps in. "Should our 'Mystery Contestant' continue to another round, the identity will continue to be concealed during the entire competition. I cannot fathom the amount of planning that goes into planning and carrying out this 'Mystery Contestant' in this year's Homerun Derby.

"Fans are encouraged to use #HRDerbyMystery to post guesses regarding this player's identity."

"And the MLB Twitter account will tweet polls for fan voting and the results at the end of each round tonight."

"Follow along on Twitter @MLB."

"Cameras are ready, the entire front panel is removed, we can only see a shadow, and it's time for the first pitch."

My eyes are glued on the silhouette-outline as the player swings and sends the ball soaring over the centerfield fence for homerun number one.

"It's Hamilton!" I turn to Alma while hopping up and down. "Hamilton's the mystery contestant." I frantically open Twitter on my phone and tweet.

Alma states there's no way I should know in one swing. I inform her, he's left-handed, and hips and left elbow positions during the swing and follow through are Hamilton's. She smiles, still not convinced.

"You are my witness when he calls later tonight, I knew after his first homerun."

We continue to watch as the 'Mystery Contestant' racks up twelve homeruns in the first round before the fourth white screen is repositioned and slowly walks down the foul line to the secure location behind the outfield bullpen.

Repeating the twelve homeruns in the second round the 'Mystery Contestant' qualifies for the finals. He will be representing the National League. I only look at Alma knowing this further proves my case that it's Hamilton.

Hamilton's FaceTime call arrives at 10:30 pm. Liberty long tucked into bed, I answer the phone as I walk toward Alma in the kitchen.

"Seriously?" I greet. "You kept that a secret from me? Your number one fan?" I position Alma in the camera with me. "I told Alma it was you after your first swing."

Alma assures Hamilton I did immediately claim it was him. She chats for a bit before turning in for the night. I continue the rest of our conversation while sitting propped against the head of my bed.

Hamilton claims if he took batting practice as often as other position players he would not have run out of steam during the finals. I assure him his ten homeruns in the final round were awesome. He only lost by five. I encourage him to read the social media posts following the big reveal of his identity.

Hamilton confesses he's been shown a few already. I hear someone talking loudly near him.

"Hey Mady, I need to let you go. I'll text you later. If you're still up, then I'll call you."

17

HAMILTON

I scowl at my agent for interrupting my call with Madison. I've jumped through his hoops all day—I need my personal time now. We walk towards our waiting transportation while he prattles on and on regarding my rising star-power, the new endorsement contacts tonight, and all of the appointments he will need to set up in the next two weeks.

When the outer stadium door opens, I'm not prepared for the number of fans still standing behind the barricades over two hours after the event. I've been spotted by those standing nearest the exit. I estimate one-hundred fans now yell my name in hopes of directing my attention towards them for autographs and selfies. Of course, they aren't yelling in unison—the noise is unnerving. Seems with 'rising star-power' comes new fans and thus less personal space and time.

I smile and wave but refuse to approach them. With the size of this crowd I'd be here several more hours if I began shaking hands, signing autographs, and posing for pictures. I respect fans—I know without them the league would not be what it is today. I'm exhausted and need to focus on tomorrow's game.

We follow the two bulky event staff t-shirt wearing men to our waiting SUV.

My agent waxes poetically at my skyrocketing star-power and all of the money it will bring our way. All I see is my current struggles with personal time, friends, and personal space growing smaller and smaller. I only trust a few in my inner-circle. Too many want to exploit me for their own personal gain. I learned in my first months in Chicago how cruel fame can be. Quick photos with female fans in public were leaked by the woman to the press claiming to be my current girlfriend or even my new fiancé. Complete strangers seek attention my fame can spark for them.

After only three months in the majors, during my first off-season a female fan with a picture at my side claimed to be carrying my baby. My agent found me a publicist and after days of emphatically stating I hadn't hooked-up with a girl since I left Athens, they went to work proving her allegations false. From that event on, I trusted only my agent, publicist, and a few teammates.

Any thoughts of dating I might have had evaporated that day. I witness my teammates and other players cheat on wives, enjoy random hook-ups, and constantly fight battles with pregnancy scares. They claim great sex is worth the hassle. I blame it on my rural Missouri small-town values. I believe in love and trust. I need to trust someone before I can share sex with them.

As we pull up to the hotel, swarms of press and paparazzi poise themselves near the entrance awaiting our arrival. I strap on my public persona, step from the SUV, and share my smile as I briskly enter the hotel.

The hotel lobby is busy for after eleven on a weeknight. While waiting for our elevator I notice several impeccably dressed women. No doubt they hope to snag more than just my eye tonight. I breathe an audible sigh of relief once the elevator sweeps us toward my room.

"Better get used to it, you've earned nationwide notoriety tonight."

My agent's words trigger bile to rise in my throat. I love playing ball. I leave everything on the field each game. I pour my heart and soul into my pitching. I love the game but hate all that comes with it. I text Madison as I lock my hotel room door. I promised to reach out to her when I could—I need to hear her voice tonight.

After an hour with no text reply from Madison, I make my peace with not performing my pregame rituals tonight, I give in to my need for sleep, and dream about the girl that holds all of my trust and owns my heart.

18

MADISON

After dinner Alma, Liberty, McGee, and I head out for our evening walk through our neighborhood. The late-August evenings are cooler now, so we no longer need to wait until later to walk. We chat with some neighbors and McGee barks when dogs bark at him. We are gone about forty minutes when we turn the corner and our house comes into view.

Alma's elbow gently bumps my arm. I look away from McGee and follow her eyes. Bethany is sitting in our porch swing.

Bethany is here in Columbia. She didn't call me, instead she drove all the way here. Fear fills me. My legs weigh a ton as I approach. Her red eyes and blotchy face alert me the reason Bethany's here is not a pleasant one.

Alma takes the stroller from my hands while still leading McGee. They say hi as they pass Bethany and continue into the house. I slowly take a seat in the swing before saying hello to my friend. I don't ask if everything is alright. I know it isn't—Bethany would not be here without Troy if it were. I lay my hand on her forearm.

"I just hopped in my car needing to take a drive." She sniffles. "I didn't have a plan." She gulps in a breath. "Next thing I knew, I was halfway here." Bethany wipes tears from her puffy red eyes and dabs her running nose on her sleeve.

"What happened honey? Does Troy know where you are?" Several scenarios stream through my mind.

"I made a special dinner last night for the two of us. I waited for quite a while before I told Troy my period started. I wanted to tell him as soon as he walked in the door. But did my best to wait until halfway through the meal." Again, she wipes her tears and gasps for breath. "He tried to be nice about it, he really did. He told me he isn't ready to try again. Can you believe that? I'm the one that suffered the pain, the trauma and I am ready. How can he not be ready?"

I don't answer. I don't know enough to answer yet. I'm not sure how to proceed here. I'm thankful Alma is inside if I need more help.

"The doctor told both of us we could have sex two weeks after the miscarriage. I've tried to sleep with my husband every week since. It's clear Troy is avoiding sex. What kind of husband won't have sex with his wife?" Again, her sleeve wipes her face. Her lower lip now quivers, and she blubbers.

"Bethany, I think he is still scared. He may just need a little more time. It had to be scary seeing someone he loves so much bleeding and in pain." I need her to know I am on her side, but support Troy here, too. "You really need to be with Troy talking this out right now. Running away just puts it off, you need to talk honestly with each other. Maybe you should call Troy right now and let him know where you are and that you are safe."

"I can't," her voice quakes. "I need some time before I talk to him. I just can't." She runs her fingers through her hair while staring at the top of the porch.

"May I call him and let him know you made it here safely and that you will talk to him tomorrow?" *Please agree* I chant to myself. Although loyal to Bethany, I feel caught in the middle right now.

"I just need a distraction that's why I went for a drive. I just wanted to think about something else for a while. I didn't plan on driving all the way to Columbia." A loud, frustrated groan rises from her chest. "Can I stay here tonight, just hang out, relax, and let you distract me? I don't want Troy to worry about me, but I think I need some time away."

I pull my phone from my back pocket, search for Troy's name in my contacts, and call. I squeeze Bethany's hand before I stand from the porch swing walking out into the front yard. I can understand Bethany needing to forget about the current situation in her life for a bit. When Troy answers, I immediately state that Bethany is here in Columbia and safe. He states he's been calling and texting for the past two hours. I'm farther away from Bethany, now.

"She's upset, hurt, asked to spend the night, and for me to distract her from her reality for an evening. I think she just needs some time away to cope. We'll take good care of her and I'll be sure she calls you tomorrow afternoon." I murmur quietly.

"Take care of her for me. I can't believe she left me," his voice breaks.

"Troy, she didn't leave you. She said she went for a quiet drive and didn't plan to end up driving all the way here. She hasn't left you, she's just trying to process everything. I think she just needs a bit to catch her breath."

Troy thanks me again and ends the call. I pause a moment before I remove the phone from my ear to return to Bethany. She is no longer crying and has no tears, just blotchy face, and red puffy eyes.

"Troy knows you are safe and sound. He asked me to take good care of you. Would you like to come inside?"

Fuck a duck! Like a punch to the gut, all air vacates my lungs. It is not until this very moment that it hits me Bethany is here and saw my daughter. My extreme worry for Bethany prevented me from thinking of this before now. Bethany saw Liberty. My secret is no more. When she comes inside, when she spends the night, she will meet Liberty. She will know.

19

MADISON

Bethany rises from the porch swing with a small smile upon her face. My heart rapidly pounds inside my chest, I am light-headed, and my palms are sweaty as I open the door. Alma sits near the front door in her reading chair book in hand. Libby is on her blanket, arms fully extended, chest and head held up, looking my way, a huge drooling smile on her face.

Alma doesn't rise from her chair. "Bethany it is so nice to see you in person. I hope your drive was good."

"Thank you," Bethany responds a large smile upon her face. "It feels like I've been here many times before. I love our video calls." She leans to her left peeking around me. "Who is this precious baby girl?"

Alma looks to me. I only have a moment to decide to share the truth or lie stating we are babysitting. "This is Liberty." I scoop her into my arms. "Libby this is mommy's friend, Bethany." I turn her back against my chest to face our guest. Libby's arms extend toward Bethany.

"May I?" Bethany asks, extending her arms and I pass Liberty to her. "Aren't you just the most precious baby girl ever? Yes, you are. Yes, you are." Bethany's sadness quickly morphs to happy baby talk.

The two sit on the blanket where Bethany offers a plastic teething ring decorated with Teddy bears to Libby.

Unsure what to do, I awkwardly choose a seat near Alma. After long, nervous moments Bethany turns her attention to me. "She looks like her father." That's all she says. She wears no smile, no sign of being mad. It's a statement. My face wears my confusion.

"She has Hamilton's dark curly hair and his beautiful brown eyes." She smiles at me. "I'm right aren't I?" I nod. "You really fooled us when we talked about his actions at the reception."

I prepare to explain, but Alma jumps in. "Bethany do you like grilled hamburgers?" When she nods, Alma excuses herself to the kitchen to fix dinner. I know she is giving me time to confess everything to my friend.

"You've been keeping your daughter from all of us. Why?" With Libby in her lap facing me, Bethany moves a bit closer.

"No one knows, not even Hamilton." I pause for a shocked reaction but see none. "On Hamilton's last night in Athens we were together—it was only the one night. Then he went to Des Moines and I didn't see him again until Adrian's wedding. I wasn't lying when I told you I didn't see him in the off-season." The tilt of Bethany's head and her smirk let me know she still thinks it is a lie if even by omission.

"I freaked the end of July when I took the pregnancy test. I knew Hamilton would drop everything, return to the farm, and take care of me and our baby. Bethany, I couldn't be the reason he gave up on his dream. He is talented. He deserves to play Major League Baseball—I couldn't ruin that."

"He wouldn't have seen you as ruining anything. Hamilton loves you, he'd love a baby the two of you created even more, it wouldn't have been your fault."

I shake my head. "I met with my college advisor, she suggested I meet Alma, and so here we are. I plan to tell Hamilton everything at the end of this season. I just wanted to allow him enough time to settle in baseball in hopes he might continue even after I introduce the two of them." I hope Bethany understands.

"She's gorgeous and you gave her such a pretty name. Liberty Armstrong." Bethany looks to me for confirmation I gave our daughter Hamilton's last name before she picks Libby up pecking her on each cheek. Baby talk returns. "So, you are the reason your mommy didn't allow video calls for several months. She's so sneaky. Yes, she is."

I love the happiness Libby brings out in my friend. Bethany's struggles this past month banish as the light that I now see returns to her eyes.

"When is your birthday?" Bethany asks my daughter.

"March 10th," I answer.

"Five months old, Libby you're a big girl like your daddy aren't you. You're gonna be tall just like your daddy." Bethany stops baby-talk and looks my way. "Adrian is going to kick your butt for this. You know that, right?" she laughs. Yes, my friend laughs for the first time since the miscarriage and it's because I'm going to be in big, big, BIG trouble with our blunt and bossy friend, Adrian. When her laughter fades she states Libby seems like a happy baby.

"She really is very easy going. Our only major issue was really for me more than her. When I returned to my spring classes, I struggled with her three-hour nursing schedule. I attempted to pump twice between my morning and then my afternoon classes on campus. It was difficult. Add to that the constant interruption to my attempts to sleep," I still have a pit in my stomach when I think of my dilemma. "I felt like a bad mother for having to change to baby formula and stop nursing. It felt selfish. I felt like I was already letting her down in the second month of her life."

"You did the right thing. You made a decision that caused less stress on you, so you could be the best mom you could be. You're not the first woman to choose formula over breast milk." She holds Liberty up in front of us. "She's happy, she's healthy, and she has a mommy that loves her. You, my friend, are a terrific mom. I have no doubts about it."

I love her faith in me. I strive to be the best mom possible. I refuse to let her down as my mother did me. Even with money tight and my being a single parent, I spend every moment I can reading, learning, and practicing parenting for her.

"Hey, Bethany," I need to make one thing crystal clear and the sooner the better. "I need you to keep my secret until I talk to Hamilton after September. You can't tell Troy, you can't tell the girls, and you can't tell your family."

Bethany turns her attention back to the prettiest girl in the room. "Liberty please assure your mommy I can and will keep this secret. But it will cost her. I require a video call with you every week and the open invitation to come visit anytime."

"Deal," I give my friend a side-hug. "Let's go help Alma with dinner."

Bethany's overnight stay passes quickly. Liberty is only away from Bethany while sleeping. I think my baby girl has proven to be the cure for Bethany's blues. We've talked about her upcoming conversation with Troy, and how the two of them should decide mutually when to try again. She's shared her fears and how she now has hope again. She claims Liberty reminded her how much she wants a baby. She can't do it alone. She understands she needs Troy's help and support to have a family.

After lunch she excuses herself to phone Troy. In the front room I can hear her happy voice and even a giggle. When she returns, she tells me Troy is cooking for her tonight. He's planned a romantic evening for the two to talk and share everything. She's excited to return home, so I am happy for them.

On the porch, Bethany says goodbye to Alma, to Libby, and to me. She snaps a picture of the three of us to hide on her cell phone before she walks to her car. She pauses with her door in hand, turns, then she returns to kiss, hug, and say goodbye one more time to my daughter before climbing into her car and heading for Athens. I can only hope that Bethany remains strong, so she may keep my secret.

Late that evening I've tucked Libby into her crib, have the monitor next to me, and am enjoying a glass of wine with Alma as we watch the end of the Cubs game. My phone vibrates next to the baby monitor.

"Who could that be?" Alma wonders out loud.

Troy: I can never thank U enough for what U did for Bethany
Troy: I know she's not completely healed
Troy: but she seems like herself again
Me: I think she was ready & some time away did the trick
Troy: whatever your conversations were
Troy: know I can never thank U enough
Me: I know she asked to visit me more often
Me: she is always welcome
Troy: thank you, thank you, thank you
Me: please take care of her. she's still very fragile

Alma asks why I am smiling. I read Troy's texts to her. We both agree our little Libby had an effect on Bethany. We are so happy she did. We believe a higher power guided her to drive to us in Columbia.

Horrible nightmares haunt me for several days following Bethany's visit. The topics of the dreams range from another miscarriage for Bethany, me having a miscarriage instead of a healthy Liberty, and Bethany telling everyone in Athens about Liberty. I struggle to fall asleep and wake up often when I do sleep. Lack of sleep begins to disrupt my days.

20

MADISON

Bethany continues to call once a week as September draws to an end. Her mood continues to improve as she and Troy begin conversations of attempting to get pregnant in the approaching fall. McGee hints at wanting another walk, however with Hamilton on the mound tonight, it won't happen. While the Cubs bat, I let him out in the backyard. Our routine changed a bit with my being at school from 7:30 a.m.-4:00 p.m. each weekday while student-teaching. I usually spend an hour each evening reviewing my lessons for the next day. I spend most of Sunday afternoon and evening extensively planning for the week. On game nights when Hamilton is pitching, we take a shorter walk with Liberty and McGee at 4:30 p.m. then I bathe Libby, while Alma fixes dinner. We position ourselves in front of the television for a 6 or 7 o'clock ballgame unless they are on the West Coast. We watch all of Hamilton's games, which the way the Cubs are playing this season is a joy. If Hamilton isn't pitching, we no longer glue ourselves in front of the TV.

As I re-enter the living room, Libby's eyes move from the toy she holds to me. She sits on her blanket with pillows propping her up. The smile she awards me warms my heart. I wave my fingers at her.

"Da-da-da," she babbles, arms flapping.

"Yes, daddy is on TV." I grab my cell phone and begin filming. "Libby, where's daddy?"

Libby smiles. "Da-da-da-da-da." Drool spills from the corner of her mouth. Her hands holding the toy animatedly fly up and down. "Da-da-da." She loves the smiles and attention she receives thus repeats her babbles. I'm still recording.

"Her first word is da-da." Alma announces for the video.

With our excitement, we miss the next three outs Hamilton pitches.

I wait until bedtime to document her first word and the date in her baby book. I replay the video on my phone several times prior to falling asleep for the night.

21

MADISON

Tonight, I anxiously await Hamilton's promised phone call. I cut Liberty's bath time in half in hopes of laying her down before he calls. Of course, tonight would be first night, that she fusses at bedtime. Alma and I each take turns rocking her while standing and sitting. Finally, we lay her in the crib and walk away. Through the monitor we listen as she babbles until she fades to sleep only minutes before her normal bedtime.

I attempt to prepare myself for Hamilton's teasing that the Cubs are going to knock my St. Louis Cardinals out of the post-season tomorrow night. As a life-long Cardinals fan, it hurts me to say that I really want the Cubs to advance. I want Hamilton to pitch in The World Series. I'm sure any other true-blue Cardinals fan would also want this opportunity for their best friend—it just sucks that it must play out this way. The Cubs and Cardinals rivalry began long before I was born.

Hamilton's video call comes through after nine. I answer on my laptop at my desk.

"I thought you might not answer," he teases.

"Are you kidding? It's a win-win for me tomorrow night." I laugh.

"Either my best friend will pitch in The World Series or my favorite team will play in it."

"Wow, I wish it was that easy for me." I can't imagine the stress he's under as the starting pitcher in tomorrow night's matchup. This game extends or ends the season for the entire team. Although baseball is a team sport, pitchers often catch the blame, thus the reason they are awarded a wins and losses stat.

"You certainly make it look easy when you are on the mound. Alma and I are nervous especially when it's a full-count." I smile knowing he does stress about his pitching before, during, and after games.

"I've completed my entire pre-game routine for the night."

I know this means he eats his usual night before a game meal, he ensures his uniform hangs in his locker exactly as he likes it, and his ball glove will be tucked under his pillow for the night. This is his ritual that started in middle school that he still is superstitious about today.

"You've got this." I know he will have a great outing tomorrow. He's much more confident this season and his arm strength is stronger than ever. With each outing his confidence grows with the best defense behind him, and Cubs' camaraderie on and off the field.

"It's the biggest game I've ever taken the mound in. I've never faced a game in which a win means we move on and a loss means our season ends. There's a lot riding on this game. Every pitch will be vital." He runs his hands over his exhausted face. "It's a lot of pressure for everyone. Your Cardinals will not make it easy for us."

"Ham, you've wanted this game and The World Series your entire life. You've dreamt of bottom of the ninth inning, two outs, and a full-count with you on the mound. This is your moment. Trust yourself, trust your team, trust your coach, and trust your fans. You have homefield advantage. The odds are stacked in the Cubs' favor."

He chuckles while shaking his head. "Still my biggest fan, aren't you?"

"Yes, and you know if I weren't student-teaching in Columbia tomorrow, I would have found a way to be at the game." I struggle with the guilt for not taking a day off for him. I want to be there, but my future career depends on my success during student-teaching. I hope he understands my reason for missing the game. And I hope he will understand my reasons when I introduce him to Liberty in the off-season that draws nearer with every passing day.

"When you win, I'm not sure I'll ever be able to fall asleep."

"One game at a time please. It will be a long nine innings—we must win these nine innings before we think about The World Series games." His large left hand runs through his wavy, brown hair.

I remember how soft his waves felt in my fingers when his hair was much shorter over a year ago. I long to run my fingers through these even longer waves. I long for the day, after a shower with wet curly hair, I can see him and Liberty side by side. When wet, his hair forms ringlets like our daughter's—they are alike in many ways.

Hamilton's voice draws my attention back to our call. "Can you believe soon our friends may have a baby, a tiny human to be responsible for. I can't believe we are old enough to be parents, can you?"

Hamilton's words hurt. I am a parent and he is a parent—he just doesn't know it yet. I will turn his world upside down when I share Liberty. I mentally shake those thoughts away. Today is not the day for this.

"Yeah, just think in December we will have three married-couple friends, Adrian's pregnant, and by then Bethany might be, too. That will only leave Savannah, you, and me as the singles of the group."

"Speaking of being single," Hamilton's face grows serious. "Have you been on any dates?"

Seriously? I thought we were sort of a long-distance couple. I thought when he kissed me and told me he loved me that he wanted me as more than a friend. Is he asking as my friend, or as someone interested in me? I find his question as confusing as his actions at Adrian's reception. Our one night together confused me and even a year later, I grow more confused with each passing month. I have no idea where we stand. I don't know if I am in the friend-zone or not.

I school my features as best I can. "With everything I've shared about student-teaching, lesson planning, tutoring, walking at night with Alma's puppy, and Bible study when do you think I've had time to socialize or date?" I tilt my head to the side glaring his way. "How about you? Any new prospects in the arm-candy or trophy-wife area?" I throw his question right back secretly hoping he will confess his feelings for me and we might forget this game of cat and mouse he seems to be playing.

"Touché," he raises his palms out towards me on the monitor.

Of course, his answer doesn't tell me his plans or feelings. He doesn't reveal anything. I could just scream—I'm so frustrated by his actions. Soon he admits his exhaustion and we end our call. I remind him he's got this—he will do great on the mound tomorrow. I wish him good luck and say goodbye.

I hope he finds sleep faster than I do. I go over my lesson plans for the next day as my college-advisor will be observing me in the class-room. I ponder his reason for asking if I had been on a date. *Is he contemplating a date with someone in Chicago? Is that his reason for asking? I feel more confused than ever. Will I ever know where we stand or what to do?*

I'm excited to watch tomorrow night's game. I'm excited both teams have made it so far this season. I hope for Hamilton to have the game of his life. I imagine him pitching in The World Series in mere weeks. So many great things are occurring all around me, yet I focus on the darkness in my life. I don't like keeping a secret from Hamilton. It festers and grows inside me stealing the happiness I should be feeling on a daily basis. With my rambling thoughts, sleep evades me for several hours.

Later, I dream of a life Hamilton and I might have had if I told him I was pregnant from the start. Hamilton insists that Liberty and I attend the Wild Card Playoff Game. Ever superstitious he insists the two of us attend every important game during his career. In my dream, Hamilton reads a Cubs Baseball children's book while tucking in Liberty. As she sleeps he speaks to her of being his good luck charm.

Before the game, I see him at his locker. Family photos of the three of us, of Liberty playing with a rosin bag on the Wrigley pitcher's mound, and Liberty in his arms with Cubbie Bear at his side line his locker shelf. Hamilton kisses his index finger then presses it to the photo of Liberty before exiting the locker room.

I wake to pee at 4 a.m. interrupting my dream prior to the end of the game. I enjoy my dreams of our little family of three. They give me hope for our future life together if Hamilton doesn't hate me for my keeping the secret. I wish I had more of these dreams. I enjoy that I never want to wake up from.

22

MADISON

Unfortunately, it's raining outside, so we can't take Liberty and McGee for a walk. McGee doesn't like storms and stays close to Alma for protection from the thunder and lightning. At least, his fear means he isn't begging for a walk this evening.

Since tomorrow is Saturday and I am too nervous for tonight's ballgame, I opt not to give Liberty a bath—I will wait for tomorrow. This way she can bathe longer. She's grown to enjoy playing with her toys in the sink during bath time. Alma and I enjoy snapping photos of her as she smiles happily, and her face is framed by dark, tight ringlets.

I place Libby in her highchair and help Alma with our snacks. We chose several instead of a meal tonight. At the store last weekend, I admitted I would be nervous, and snacking might help me during the game. Alma then suggested nibbling instead of dinner. We take turns placing a few round cereal pieces on Libby's tray as we prepare popcorn, cereal snack mix, cheese and crackers, and chocolate chip cookies, along with our favorite fall snack of candy corn mixed with dry-roasted peanuts. We even make a small bowl of cereal rounds for Libby to enjoy during the game.

I carry several snack bowls to the coffee table while Alma places the cheese and crackers in the refrigerator next to a new bottle of wine for later. She offers to fix a cooler with drinks in it to take into the living room. I let her know I might need to walk between half-innings if I'm nervous, we opt to leave our cold snacks and beverages in the kitchen.

I scoop up my daughter, peppering kisses upon her chubby cheeks as we make our way into the living room. I set up her portable crib to keep her near for the entire game. Alma helps me record a video to put in my digital journal for Hamilton. I share our snack set-up, menu for tonight's game, and we record his littlest fan's game day attire. She wears a Cubs headband in her soft curls, a miniature Armstrong Cubs Jersey just like her daddy's, a diaper cover with Cubbie Bear on the seat, and little Cubs socks.

The pre-game show on the television discusses the Cubs and Hamilton's pitching. I point to him and prompt her to say daddy. Alma positions the camera just to the side of the TV pointed at me holding Liberty. Libby wears a huge smile wet with baby slobber. She extends her chubby little arms with wiggling fingers. "Da-da-da." One hand returns to her mouth. With two fingers inside she mumbles, "Da-da-da-da-da."

I look into the camera and inform Hamilton at seven months old, it is the only word she speaks so far. The three of us wish him luck and end this video journal entry. I place Libby on the floor seated with pillows surrounding her. I scoot her favorite toys within her reach, then place a kiss on the crown of her head. She smells of all things baby with oat cereal, and of course I love it.

I nervously munch on snack after snack as the game progresses. In the bottom of the fourth inning the score is still 0-0. Hamilton is on fire. His pitches baffle batters. He's given up only one hit. As he strikes out the next batter and we move to the top of the fifth inning, I hurry to the restroom—I don't want to miss anything.

Liberty finishes her bottle, I take her from Alma's arms and plan to rock her to sleep. Sitting in the rocker, I pull Liberty tight to my chest. "It's time for daddy's little girl to go to sleep." I kiss her temple then lay her in my arms. She extends an arm placing her hand on my chin. I love when she seeks comfort in touching me. With my free hand I lift and kiss her tiny hand. "Sweet dreams baby girl."

Libby's eyes grow heavy. Though my mind is on the game, I continue to rock her well into sleep. The Cardinals nearly score in the top of the fifth and again in the top of the sixth. Finally, the Cubs score as their clean-up hitter sends a homerun flying deep to center-field. I know that one run is not going to win this game, but it's a start. I place my sleeping girl in her portable crib near the base of the steps. Walking to the kitchen I inform Alma, "It's wine time."

Frustration builds as the Cardinals begin to get one or two base runners each inning but fail to score. In the top of the eighth inning Hamilton's fastball fades a bit. The coach makes a pitching change after one out bringing in a right-handed closer. Although he should be proud of the job he did, Hamilton's body tells me he's upset. I smile knowing Hamilton will get credit for the win if the Cubs pull out a victory.

With our wine bottle empty next to our two glasses we nervously watch as the game moves into the top of the ninth inning Cubs 1-Cardinals 0. One run is not enough of a lead to believe the Cubs have won—they need three more outs. They can't let the Cardinals score. I'm too worked up to sit. I pace from Liberty's crib to the sofa and back while my eyes remain glued on the television.

After the right-hander strikes out the fourth batter this inning, Alma and I stand holding hands facing the TV. The score is still 1-0, there are now two outs, runners occupy first and third base with the number-four batter of the Cardinals line-up approaching the plate. I nearly scream when the Cubs choose to intentionally walk this renowned homerun-hitter. My free hand covers my mouth, so I don't wake my sleeping baby. The bases are now loaded—the Cubs need only one out. There is a force out at any base. They only need to cleanly field the ball and toss it to the nearest base.

In a risky play, a pinch-hitter is brought in for the Cardinals. The pitcher winds up and throws a fastball over the corner of the plate. I squat, and tears fill my eyes as the ball leaves the bat with a trajectory sure to send it far over the left-field fence. A walk-off grand slam, my St. Louis Cardinals advance to The World Series. Hamilton and the Chicago Cubs' season is officially over until next spring.

Once the shock of the final inning of the game ebbs, I contemplate shooting a text to Hamilton. *What should one send her best friend after such a heart-breaking loss?*

Me: Good Game (No. delete, delete, delete)
Me: You threw a great game (No. delete, delete, delete)
Me: I love you (*Fuck a duck! I can't send that.* delete, delete, delete)

I stare blankly at my cell phone searching for words to comfort my friend. A tiny smile creeps on my face remembering it was a gift from Hamilton.

Me: You gave me this phone as a gift
Me: so we could be here for each other
Me: I miss you
Me: words can't express how much

Tonight, in my bedroom, I miss Hamilton more than usual. Our framed photo laughing on his tailgate rests in my hands. I recall sharing my clumsy hog lot story and his ensuing teasing. My finger traces his handsome face while I remember he gifted the framed photo to me during the scavenger hunt he created for me.

I miss this playful Hamilton. I miss the young man and the carefree times we spent together. Our former life in the small town of Athens quickly filled with work and grownup responsibilities.

I pray we will find our way back to each other. I hope fate will weave a road where we may find ourselves happy together with Liberty. While I hope we will be a couple, I pray he at least allows us to raise our daughter together.

23

MADISON

Hamilton's first full season in the MLB ended four days ago. Although I've texted him daily, I haven't heard from him. The students keep me on my toes while I am there, and I love every second of it, but I worry about him when I'm not at school. As I drive home today, I decide to call him tonight.

With no ballgames this week, Alma and I enjoy long walks each night after dinner with Liberty and McGee. On tonight's walk we enjoy our neighbors' fall and Halloween decorations. We wave as some work to rid their yards of the red, orange, and brown leaves. Luckily, we do not worry about leaves in Alma's yard as the lawncare company takes care of them once a week. McGee is content with his long walk and Libby yawns as we return home.

While I watch Libby enjoy her bath time in the kitchen sink. I shoot a quick text to Hamilton.

Me: Can you talk?

While pregnant and the seven months since I've imagined ways to let Hamilton know about Liberty. I told myself I would tell him at the end of this season. Now that his season is over, I need to figure out when and how I plan to do it. I only have from now until February to carry this out. With Thanksgiving and Christmas in there the timeframe grows smaller still. Hamilton will spend time with his sister and mother in Athens for both holidays and he likes to report early to Mesa before spring training. I watch Libby in the sink still consumed by thoughts of Hamilton.

Noticing heavy eyes and pruned fingers, I lift my girl from the water and wrap her in a fluffy towel. While she sucks the water off her hand I dry her off before dressing her for bed. I carry her to Alma for goodnight kisses. Alma lays her book on a nearby table to hold Libby in her lap for a minute.

As I carry Liberty toward the nursery, I inform Alma I plan to write in my room and bid her good night. Once fast asleep in her crib, I head to my bedroom with monitor in hand. I place the monitor on the dresser by the door. It's close enough I can see the red lights if she wakes up and far enough away it won't be heard on my call. My little girl grows fast. I mean *our* little girl. Soon she will be crawling, pulling up, talking more, and walking. I've got to talk with Hamilton —he's missing more with each passing week.

I select Hamilton's name from my favorite contacts list and dial. It's 8:15 p.m. I am not sure if he will answer. I can't imagine why he hasn't responded to my texts for four days. I nervously wait as it rings three times and I hear Hamilton's deep voice on his voicemail message.

"Hi, just checking in. I figure you are busy with end of the season winding down. I hope you're alright. Please shoot me a text when you can. Bye." I try to sound light-hearted. I don't want him to know how worried I am about him. I haven't heard from him since the Cubs loss. I worry he's being hard on himself. *Is he depressed his season is over?* It's not like him to ignore my attempts to contact him. I don't want him to know how much I miss his texts and calls.

When not with my daughter or working on lesson plans, I've begun writing again. Journaling or creating stories consumes my free time. As sleep often eludes me, I find several hours each night to place my pen to paper. After many hours pass while writing, I fall asleep with no text or call from Hamilton.

24

MADISON

I'm on my knees wailing while tears drench my cheeks, chin, and neck. As his truck pulls from Alma's driveway, my life, my entire world leaves with him. Hamilton doesn't look my direction one final time. His mother keeps her eyes on the backseat avoiding me. I scream when I no longer see his red truck.

Alma and her daughter Taylor approach with words they hope will calm me. Through my sobs I see their mouths moving, but I do not hear their words. I don't want to hear them. Nothing matters—nothing will ever matter again. My world fades to black.

I feel cold metal upon my chest. I don't open my eyes—I can't. I hear Taylor instructing another to write a prescription. I hear a male voice but can't make out his words. A cold hand brushes my hair from my face and Alma whispers near my ear to come back to her. The dark emptiness engulfs me once more.

Warm light bathes my face, I internally debate covering my eyes with a pillow or opening them. My bladder urges me to wake if only for a moment. I open one eye. My room is empty. Opening my second eye I notice not only are my curtains open, but the wood-slat blinds no longer decorate the window with horizontal lines. I'm sure it's Alma's doing.

Sitting up every muscle in my body protests. I'm unsure how long I laid in my horizontal slumber. It doesn't matter. A quick trip to my restroom, then I will return to my protective blankets and forget about the world around me.

My eyes remain on the tile floor as I enter. Upon flushing my eyes remain down as I sip water from the faucet of the sink and pad back to the bed. I don't need to see my reflection, I know how I look—I look and feel like walking death.

While my legs slide beneath the blankets, Alma darts into my room.

"I've brought water, diet cola, chocolate, crackers, and a ham sandwich." She gasps for breath. "My doctor visited yesterday morning. I've placed your pills on the tray. Taylor insists they will help."

I fluff my pillow, lay my head down, and close my eyes.

"Madison," Alma's stern tone is not one I've heard before. "You need to eat, you need to drink—it's been two days." She rips the blankets from my body. "I've allowed your hiding in bed long enough. It's time to take care of yourself. In order to fight, you need to be strong and healthy. Liberty needs you now more than ever."

25

MADISON

I bolt upright. I'm drenched head to toe. I brush my wet hair from my face as I frantically search my room. I dart from my bed to the nursery. I slap a hand over my mouth when a sob escapes at the sight of my sleeping daughter in her crib.

I pant as I attempt to take a full breath. She's here. Liberty is here with me. She's not with Hamilton. She's not in Chicago. I haven't lost custody of my daughter. It was a dream. It was a horrible dream. It was just a nightmare—my worst fears playing out in my head.

Unable to restrain myself, I lift my daughter clutching her to my chest. She remains asleep while I hold her close—we rock. The creaking of the wooden chair and her warmth at my chest calm my racing heart.

The next morning, I wake to texts.

Hamilton: sorry I missed your call
Hamilton: been in meetings with coaches & agent

Hamilton: Stan going through something
Hamilton: been hanging with him at night, too
Hamilton: promise to call soon
Hamilton: (heart emoji)

These texts rest my concerns as he sounds okay just busy. I know Stan is another Chicago player. I am not surprised Hamilton is a leader on his team and helps other players out when needed. I'm happy to hear from Hamilton—my heart is marginally lighter as I start my day.

A week later, I cringe when my cell phone vibrates on my night stand while I change into my pajamas. The game ended ten minutes ago—he waited ten minutes later than I thought he would.

Hamilton: Are you up?
Me: You know I am!
Hamilton: Testy, aren't you?

I angrily stare at the cell phone in my hand. I know he is teasing, so I fight the urge to remind him his team didn't even make it to the World Series. I can't be that mean. The Cubs came so close this year, it was very exciting for him, the team, and for the fans. I know my disappointment at my Cardinals' loss is not the same as his loss with the Cubs. I jump as my phone vibrates indicating an incoming Face-Time call in my hand.

"Hey," I hesitantly greet awaiting more teasing.

"I'm sorry."

"Don't worry about it. I'm just tired and pissed that they couldn't step up on their homefield to win. It's not your fault." I slip under my quilt with my back leaning on pillows against the headboard.

"I'm sorry for teasing you. I know better than anyone how serious you take your Cardinals. They were one run away. Sometimes being so close makes the loss even more sour." I hear rustling on the other end of the line.

"What are you doing?" In the background I see pillows and his headboard.

"I just got done watching the game with Stan." The rustling is louder for a moment then he continues. "He messed up on our last road trip, his wife found out, and he's been crashing with me ever since. You won't tell the paparazzi, will you?" he teases.

"She's warming back up to him and has let him visit the kids a few times now." Hamilton sighs. I bite my lip as he wipes his hands down his tired face then runs his hands through his dark waves. "Some guys are so stupid. They forget about the great things they have at home and go hog-wild on the road. It makes me sick to be around it all and I'm not even married."

"If you don't approve of their actions, why are you helping Stan?"

"This was his first screw-up. He hangs with the guys and drinks before turning in each night. He had too much to drink following our victory before the Wild Card game. I guess when you hang around those type of guys, eventually you imitate their actions. Hold on a second." I hear a thump as he places the phone on something and I can only see a lampshade, then more rustling. I imagine him removing his shirt in that one-arm-above-the-head way guys do. When I begin daydreaming of his muscles and chest I reprimand myself for such thoughts.

"He came to my hotel room at 3:00 a.m. He was a mess—he immediately regretted his actions. We talked for hours not getting any sleep that night. He chose to come clean—he just waited until our season ended. Now he is paying the price." Hamilton makes a stretching sound. He's lying shirtless in bed now. I struggle to keep my thoughts on our conversation and not my desire to lie beside him. "I give it another week or two and she'll invite him to move back home. I don't mind having him here, but I'll be glad when I have the place to myself again."

I like the dark sexy scruff covering his jaws and chin. It's more than a five o'clock shadow but he's kept it groomed. I imagine it grazing my neck, my chest, and my thighs. When I slowly raise my free hand up to touch him, I snap my thoughts back to the present and our conversation. I scramble for something to say to keep my thoughts off the reactions my body has for my very sexy friend.

"Stan's got to be putting a damper on your entertaining the ladies." I tease hoping he does no such thing. But I know he is an athlete, he's famous, he's super sexy, he's single, and he's a man with needs. He's not a single-parent like me curbing my needs to earn my degree and care for our daughter.

"Right, I have no free time. Plus, I see the strain it puts on all relationships with all of our appearances and travel."

When he pauses, I jump in. "There are these things called no-strings-attached hook-ups." I slap my hand to my forehead. *What am I doing?* I want him. I want to be the one he wants. *Why am I suggesting he hook-up with random women?* I hate when my mouth moves before my brain filters the words.

His laughter tickles my ears. "Did you just slap yourself?"

Fuck a duck! He saw that? I am such an idiot. I'm still a novice when it comes to smartphones and relationships. He is so out of my league.

"Yeah, I thought a bug was about to bite me." Nice. Real nice. I'm in my bedroom and it's late October. Bugs have gone into hiding like I wish I could right now. Hamilton's laughter continues causing warmth to flood my body despite my embarrassment.

"I'm not like the others. I don't want paparazzi posting photos of me in print and on all of the gossip sites. Other players don't mind a different girl every week, but I like my privacy. I am not a playboy, and do not want to be portrayed that way. It's just easier to avoid it all." I watch as he changes positions. *Is he trying to kill me with all of the noises he's making while seeing him chest bare in his bed?*

"I guess I'm truly a small-town guy. I'm not interested in making myself available to a total stranger. Some of the women that flock around us are trying to hook themselves to a star. They stop at nothing. A few guys have kids in cities we travel to because they chose one night with a woman wanting an athlete to take care of them for the rest of their lives. It's so much worse than I imagined and heard about before being called up." Hamilton speaks through his yawn. "I find it hard to trust anyone. It's nothing like Athens, you know?"

"Yeah. Columbia is different, but nothing like the world you live in." His yawn causes me to yawn.

"How's your social life?"

"Right now, it consists of chatting online with fellow student-teachers about our placements and lesson planning. I'm finding a teacher can work from the moment they get home until the moment they give up to go to bed and still feel like they didn't get enough done."

"Let me rephrase my question," he chuckles. "Other than all things college and student-teaching how's the social life?"

"I still attend Bible study on Wednesday nights. We occasionally plan an outing like a movie or bowling for the weekend. Alma and I walk McGee each night and we talk with the neighbors. I've been invited to drinks on Friday's at four when we leave school by a few of the teachers at the middle school. I plan to go next week, although I am the only one not twenty-one yet." I shrug. I know they believe I am the usual college senior at age twenty-two or twenty-three. I don't like to flaunt my ability to move through my college classes faster than usual. "I'll be the only one ordering a tea with lemon."

"You should still go. It might lead into a good reference or them putting in a good word for you when you are applying for teaching positions." He's right—it's the reason I even considered going in the first place. Finding a job post-graduation is all about networking and putting myself out there. "Any dating?"

"Ham, I'm so hyper-focused on my student-teaching that I haven't given it a thought." It's a lie—I think about dating Hamilton every time I look at my daughter and while I lie in bed at night. "Besides, I am still young. There will be plenty of time to find Mr. Right after

December." Speaking these words out loud puts a bad taste in my mouth.

Hamilton yawns again.

"You look like you need some sleep."

"I thought when the season ended, I'd be free to visit Athens and you down in Columbia. My agent has me booked for the next three weeks. We are meeting with companies for possible endorsement deals like Gatorade, Snickers Bars, Nike, a local car dealership, and a few more. The Cubs Organization has me making several appearances at area events and fundraisers. I even get to visit the children's ward at a local hospital and a few inner-city programs. I've been leaving the condo by nine and arriving back after six each day when I don't have a dinner meeting to attend. I'm not sure when it will slow down. My agent reminds me it's increasing my income and provides job security. I'm just ready for a vacation."

I mentally panic at his mention of coming down to Columbia. We need to arrange a time together as I plan to divulge my secret, but I can't have him just pop-in. I'm a bit relieved it seems he is too busy to plan a time for us to meet right now. I'll try to plan something when his world slows down in the months to come.

"Promise me you'll give me notice when you plan to visit Athens. I want to find time in my schedule to see you." I hope this will allow me to keep him away from Columbia until I have a chance to talk with him about our daughter.

"I promise," he speaks through a yawn. "I better let you go, you have school tomorrow and I have meeting after meeting."

"Try to get more rest, you look exhausted. I don't want you running yourself down and getting sick." I cringe at my nagging him.

"Okay, mom," he teases. "Sweet dreams."

I'm sure they will be sweet dreams of you, I think to myself as I place my phone back on the charger and switch off my lamp.

26

MADISON

Saturday is currently my favorite day. I don't even mind that I am awake by 7:00 a.m. It's my day to enjoy my daughter. I don't pick up my laptop or look at lesson plans the entire day —we fill our day with mommy-daughter activities. Currently we are in my bed chatting about our plans for today. I love her babbles. I ask a question and she answers me. It doesn't matter that I have no idea what she attempts to say.

"Should we go downstairs and make breakfast for Alma?"

"Da-ba-ba-ta-da," Liberty responds with arms and legs animatedly signaling her excitement.

When I rise from the bed, Libby lifts her arms to signal for me to pick her up. I scoop her into my arms and smoother her with kisses causing baby giggles to erupt. I have not a care in the world in these moments.

I secure Liberty in her highchair, place a few cereal rounds and two teethers on her tray, then speak to her often as I start the coffee and prepare the griddle for bacon. I look forward to a long walk to the park today, I will swing and slide with her as Alma takes photos and McGee enjoys the dog park. We are blessed with a sixty-five-degree day this first weekend in November—we must enjoy the weather while we can. Maybe we will eat a picnic lunch in the back yard, too. The fresh air will quickly wear out McGee and Liberty. I'll help Alma around the house while she naps. I live for these simple days.

"La-La," Liberty announces Alma's arrival in the kitchen loudly. McGee scurries to eat the cereal she knocked off her tray in her excitement.

"Good morning Miss Libby," Alma greets before pouring her cup of coffee. Libby jabbers right back to her with a piece of cereal visible on her tongue.

While my Saturday with Liberty allows me to genuinely smile and enjoy myself, as night falls my thoughts darken and all of the troubles in the world creep in. My thoughts move from troubled students, to miscarriages, to my mother, to my father's death, to the loss of my girlfriends and Hamilton, to my ever on my mind secret, to starving families, then to other atrocities from the nightly news.

As is my new habit, I bleed my feelings into my notebook each night. The lined white paper quickly fills with my treacherous thoughts. My remembering that today is my mother's birthday cut me open after Liberty's bath time. I've looked forward to tonight's writing for two hours now. I've needed to banish my thoughts onto the paper.

I spill every drop—I rid myself one by one. Tears stream as I confess my continued love for her after everything. I admit the guilt I carry for not trying harder to get her help. I should have enlisted the help of adults to force her into treatment at a rehab facility. I should have begged our family doctor to have her committed. As her daughter I should never have given up—I should have fought for her over and over to seek the help she needed.

Thoughts turn into words. Words form sentences and sentences form a story on paper. The younger version of me becomes my main character. Certain aspects of my life mirror the character while in many ways we are different. Page after page the story flows, grows, and with it my heart grows lighter. This is my therapy.

27

MADISON

Wednesday, Alma's three children with spouses and kids arrive to celebrate Thanksgiving. The full house is chaotic. As an only child it's a bit overwhelming. The siblings seem to have adopted me as a little sister. The children love Liberty and she enjoys little humans to entertain her, as well as, a second dog in the house.

I attempt to help Alma with the cooking but find her two daughters and daughter-in-law are much more proficient than me. I opt to help setting the table, corralling the kids, caring for the dogs, and taking care of the dishes. I take turns sitting at the kids' table with Liberty and the adult table at meal times. Taylor's two pre-teen daughters love caring for Libby. They claim they are practicing at babysitting.

While Alma, her oldest daughter Taylor, and youngest daughter Cameron begin work on the big meal Thursday morning after breakfast; her daughter-in-law Ava and I peel potatoes at the kitchen table.

Taylor informs our group, "My daughters are hinting they want a baby brother or sister now, thanks Madison." Sarcasm laces her voice.

"I think that is a lovely idea," Alma quickly responds.

"Seriously?" Taylor looks offended. "My daughters are almost grown, my career is on the rise, and soon we will have the house to ourselves. Why start all over with night feedings, diapers, and teething? I'd be fifty-eight when he or she would graduate high school. No thank you. They can just babysit and visit Libby to get their baby fix."

I chuckle. Both of Alma's daughters and her son are work-a-holics. Taylor meticulously planned the birth of her daughters barely twelve months apart after her two years of residency and prior to focusing on her cardio-thoracic specialty. Cameron is still single at thirty-years-old. She's an editor with a large publishing house in Dallas, Texas. She works long hours and frequently travels.

"It's Cameron's turn to give you grandbabies," Taylor informs Alma. "Trenton and I gave you two girls and two boys. It's time she marries and spits out some little ones." Taylor winks at me.

"First, I will not 'spit out' anything let alone a tiny human. You know for a physician you sure don't talk like one. Mom, I think you wasted money on her education." Cameron addresses Alma with the voice of a true youngest-child. "Second, I don't have to marry to have a baby. When I'm ready, I'll just have one."

Alma's sharp intake of breath and hand to her chest alarm me. I worry she doesn't feel well. Cameron on the other hand, knows exactly what her reaction means. "Mom, I want nothing more than to meet Mr. Right, marry, and start a family. I need to inform you, finding Mr. Right is more difficult than walking through land mines. I seem to find the creeps and phychos. So, if I feel the strong urge to start my family, I'll take care of it myself if a good male candidate isn't in the picture." Cameron smiles knowing this will not set well with her family.

"You must be looking in the wrong places. Have you tried online dating or Tinder?" Alma stands with hands on hips attempting to solve a problem for her youngest child.

"Mom!" Taylor shouts astonished.

Ava beside me spews her mouthful of iced tea all over the potatoes we've peeled on the table.

Cameron simply looks to heaven asking, "Why me?"

"How do you know what Tinder is?" All three women look my way instead of at Alma.

"Don't look at me, I didn't teach her about that app."

"Please," Alma addresses her children. "I watch television and movies, I read, I'm an educated woman, and I keep up on the latest trends. Besides two women in my Bible Study were chatting about their sons using Tinder to avoid long-term relationships and how they fear they will never have grandchildren. I came home and Googled it." She points to Taylor and then to Cameron. "Your mother isn't ready to be put out to pasture yet."

Ava and I rinse the potatoes of her iced tea, then continue peeling. I love Alma's ability to still surprise her daughters. I've often thought of her as twenty-five-year-old brain in her sixty-five-year-old body.

"Just so you know Tinder is for one-night-stands, mom, not finding a long-term mate." Taylor states returning to her pie crust.

I excuse myself to check on Liberty while the women continue instructing Cameron on how to find a man. Libby sits on her blanket, she has a toy in her hand, I notice her head is bobbing slightly, when I am close I also note her heavy eyelids. My little girl needs a nap. The constant attention from the four other kids and two dogs is sensory overload for such a little girl. She lifts her little arms and hands toward me. I scoop her into my arms and we escape to the quiet of her nursery. Her head lays heavily on my shoulder up the stairs and into her room. While I change her diaper, she yawns and rubs her eyes with her chubby little fists.

Although she falls asleep quickly, I choose to rock her for several more minutes. I love Alma's family and am happy everyone came to visit. But I'm off from school and I have very little time with Liberty as they all take their turns. I plan to steal a few loves right now. In here, I don't have to make sure I smile at appropriate times—I don't have to fake happiness. I let my guard down and enjoy my daughter.

I play with a few of her stray ringlets—I'm happy she has Hamilton's dark curls. I gently run my fingertip over her eyebrows and little nose. She's growing too fast. I can't believe how big she is in my arms now. My baby is eight months old and crawling. This little one is very active as she explores and keeps Alma and me on our toes every day.

I place Liberty in her crib, turn on the monitor, and a sound machine, before I shut off the light and close her door.

28

MADISON

I find Cameron sitting on the top step, so I join her placing the baby monitor beside me. "Have enough advice from the married women?" I tease.

"They mean well," she states. "I wanted a few minutes to chat with you."

I'm caught off guard. I have no idea why she wants to chat with me.

"First, you must promise not to be mad." Cameron looks sternly my way. When I nod, she continues. "Mom shared two of your stories with me, you are a gifted writer."

"Wait, what?" *Her mom? Alma? She did what with my stories?* In late-September I began going through my old notebooks full of young-adult stories. The urge to write again was strong, so I purchased ten new notebooks, and shared a couple of my previously written stories with Alma.

"You promised not to be mad." Cameron sternly reminds me. "She told me you shared them with her. She loved them and shared them with me. You *are* a *gifted* writer. Mom says you haven't sent inquiries to agents or to publishing houses, is that true?"

"Umm," my mind still tries to process Alma's betrayal and

Cameron's words. I shared four of the stories I've written over the past three years for fun. I mentioned it during one of the days we read while it rained outside. She insisted I let her read them. I never thought she would share them with someone. I sure didn't think she would share them with her daughter, an editor at a publishing house in Dallas.

"They are in my suitcase. I made a few, and I mean a very few edits and suggestions for you." When I don't react, she continues. "I think you should let me pitch them at next month's new authors' meeting. I'm confident one of our three publishing houses will pick them up." She turns my chin to face her. "You're mad. You can't be mad—you promised. You really have no idea how good they are, do you? Madison, readers *need* these books. The young-adult market needs more authors like you."

She places her hands on each of my shoulders, arms fully extended as she stares at my face. "I need you to hear me. I need your permission to pitch your books. I'd love to see your other stories, too. They are *much* too good to hide in a drawer or in a laptop file. Your students need these books. Let me help you, please."

"You really think kids would enjoy reading them?" I can't wrap my mind around her positive words on my writing. I transformed my thoughts and fears into stories as a form of therapy for me. I never intended to share them.

"Madison, yes your writing *is that* good."

"I write as a hobby at night when I can't sleep. I've always kept journals and even written some poems. I can't believe you are sitting here telling me you, an editor, want to pitch my stories. I mean, I've daydreamed about it a couple of times, but it was never something I planned to pursue."

"I'm not promising anything. I've worked with hundreds of writers, I've edited many manuscripts, and I believe your work is among the best I've seen. I am confident you'll find others interested in them. I work for the parent company—we have two smaller publishing houses that we also own. If you permit me to pitch these first two books, I feel one of the three houses will pick them up." Cameron's smile is infectious.

I am excited that she enjoyed them. I even feel hopeful that someone else might like them well enough to publish them. My stories contain characters based on little parts of me. In my seven stories I've written about the topics of an alcoholic parent, of losing a parent, of a smart girl attempting to not appear so smart around her peers, and of a nerd that wants to be in the popular crowd. All of my stories are based in one middle school with three different groups of friends. Writing about my life is therapeutic for me—maybe my books can help others in similar situations. Maybe Cameron really can help me. A hundred questions form in my mind.

"Let's take some time tonight after Libby goes to bed to go over the two I have. If you choose, you can rewrite and share an electronic file with me. I will print copies of the manuscript to share at the meeting. Then we will just wait and see if we hear anything the following week or two. When they pick up a new author it happens quickly. They call, set up meetings, explain the timeline, and the process. You will know before Christmas either way."

I agree to work with her later tonight. While Cameron returns down to the family, I remain on the step. I love Alma. I consider myself blessed to spend each day with her. However, at this moment, I'm still hurt. The fact that she didn't ask when she knew how private I kept them hurts. I know if she asked me, I most likely would have given my permission to share my stories with Cameron. I know it's the same outcome as if she did ask first. Cameron's reaction and confidence in my stories would still have surprised me. I know Alma only wants the best for me—I guess I can't fault her for that.

I allow myself a few moments to process the fear, the excitement, and to dream. I imagine two of my books get published. I envision local school and city libraries carrying my book. A bud of excitement blooms. I like the idea of being published. With Cameron's help it just might happen. My thoughts fade as my phone vibrates.

Hamilton: how's the crowded house?

Me: busy

Hamilton: wish u were here

Me: tell your mom & sis I say hi

Hamilton: we consider u family, too

Hamilton: I should have insisted u join us

Me: already made plans with Alma when u asked

Me: your family likes u all to themselves

Me: they don't see u enough

Hamilton: I don't see u enough

Me: when do u head back to Chicago?

Hamilton: Friday evening

Hamilton: 2 more weeks then calendar opens up

Me: maybe then we can get together

Me: I'm done teaching

Me: I just observe until Dec. 5th then graduation

Hamilton: I'll call Monday

Hamilton: & we'll get something on calendar

Me: I'll be very honored

Me: Hamilton Armstrong's calendar (heart emoji)

Hamilton: Stop

Hamilton: u r more important than events on calendar

Hamilton: I hope you know that (heart emoji)

Hamilton: I have to do these appearances

Hamilton: I want to see you

Hamilton: big difference

Me: (Heart emoji)

Me: Alma needs my help. we'll be eating soon

Me: enjoy your family

Hamilton: (Heart emoji)

Me: (2 Heart emojis)

With the busy house, the big meal, and Cameron's bomb about my books; I don't need to worry about an approaching get together with Hamilton to tell him he has a daughter. His proclamation of missing me and being more important than events on his calendar further confuses me. I have enough on my plate today and tomorrow. I decide to wait for the weekend to worry about Hamilton, his feelings, my feelings, and a December you're-a-daddy meeting.

29

HAMILTON

Sitting at the Thanksgiving table, I look from my mother, to my sister, to the empty chair. I should have contacted Madison in October. Then she would be sitting at our table, enjoying my mother's extravagant Thanksgiving meal.

We are her family. Since 8th grade Madison has been at our holiday table and a member of our family. I can't fault her for spending time with Alma's family. I abandoned her. We planned to attend college together and I bailed. In the hours after I was drafted I changed our plans and left her on her own for college. With no support from her mother and no other family she started a new chapter of her life without me.

My mother's voice draws my attention. "We miss her, too."

I realize I was staring at the empty chair Madison occupied every Thanksgiving, Christmas, and Easter for five years. I thought she would always be here, my friend, my adopted little sister. Although my feelings for Madison have changed, I still believe she belongs at our family table for the holidays. It's time for me to lay my heart out and share *all* of my feelings with Madison. If I want to share every part of my life with her, she needs to know before she applies for teaching positions after her quickly approaching college graduation.

My mother shares all she's learned about Madison's relationship with Alma and her children. Mom, through her many emails and phone conversations each week with Madison, knows more than I do. I'm glad Madison has found a safe family to live with while in Columbia but need her to know this family needs and misses her, too.

My mom clutches my left hand upon the table. "She knows we wish she was here."

Her words don't calm my thoughts. They only fortify my resolve to open up to Madison. I can't let another off-season pass without spending time ensuring Madison knows exactly how I feel, and I need her by my side.

30

MADISON

Me: R U awake?
Hamilton: Yeah, what's up?
Me: I have too much on my mind
Hamilton: Want me to call?

I hesitate in my response. I would love to talk to him about everything but hearing his voice over the phone before bed will just add more thoughts, although very pleasant thoughts, to my long list to worry about. Maybe he can distract me from everything else.

"Hey," I greet when he answers my call.

"Hi, why didn't you video call?"

"Are you crazy? It's after eleven on Thanksgiving night. We've been up and cooking since seven. I've chased dogs and kids most of the day. I'm exhausted, my hair is in a messy bun, and I'm in my pajamas."

"None of that matters to me and you know it. I've seen you..."

I want it to matter. I want him to desire me, to find me sexy, to think I am beautiful, and at this moment I am anything but beautiful.

"Spill it," his deep gravelly voice prompts. "What has your mind swimming instead of sleeping?"

I share how much Alma loves having her family here for the holiday weekend and how they've somewhat adopted me as a little sister. For an only child it is both comforting and overwhelming. I tell Hamilton about the four resumes and applications I've submitted for open teaching positions in the spring in the Columbia area. I convey my worry that I will have to wait until fall to find one. I share my conversation with Cameron about my books. Hamilton knows I write to relax and work through things in my life. He's very excited that I might be published. I speak of Bethany, Troy, her new pregnancy, and that she is keeping it from Troy. I'm both excited and scared for them. She so desperately wants to start a family. Then I talk about Adrian's pregnancy and the approaching wedding of Latham and Salem.

I leave out my confusion at his actions. *Am I his friend? Or am I more?* I also do not share that I have a life-altering secret I need to share with him and I'm worried how he will react. I don't reveal my insomnia is back and I fear the darkness of depression is creeping in again.

"So, you can see I have many reasons I can't fall asleep tonight." I roll onto my side with my cell phone between the pillow and my ear, then turn off the bedside lamp.

"You've always worried too much about those around you. You can't solve everything for everyone and I love your loyalty to family and friends. Let's focus on Madison's items in your list." He is both stern and caring.

"Have you applied to school districts outside of the Columbia Metro Area?" *I wonder if his question includes areas very far from the Columbia area, like Athens.* "I've only applied in the metro so far. As it is mid-year, most districts won't have openings until late-spring and summer when contract renewals occur." I don't share that I have free childcare and living accommodations here versus me moving to another town.

"Remind me again what endorsements you have."

Endorsements? Have I spoke of these enough that he remembers? It's not usually a term those outside of education use. "I can teach in Kindergarten through eighth grade. I have endorsements in Social Studies and Mathematics. I'd love to find a history or math job in a middle school." I roll to my back, once again holding my phone in my hand. Staring at my dark ceiling *I wonder if he is doing the same in his room. Is he in pajamas or just boxers? Is his chest bare? Stop it! Focus Madison!*

"I only have seven school days left in my student-teaching," I sigh before yawning. "I think I am too attached to my students. I will have spent fourteen weeks with these middle schoolers and I already dread never seeing them again."

"This is what will make you an excellent teacher. You care about their learning, their development, and them as people. The students lucky enough to get you as a teacher are blessed." His faith in my teaching abilities causes me to smile. He is my number one fan, just as I am his.

"I'm sure like anything else, it's a numbers game. The more resumes and applications you send, the calls for interviews will start rolling in." I hear his yawn through the phone prompting me to yawn. "Think back to middle and high school. Did we have a single teacher that graduated from the University of Missouri?" While I think he continues. "All of our teachers attended Missouri Western, Northwest Missouri, and Truman State—all excellent teaching programs but not the University of Missouri. I have to believe your degree will set you apart from other applicants when you apply outside of Columbia."

I had not thought of that. *Why does he keep mentioning for me to apply outside of Columbia? He's not in Athens.* We shared a desire to leave and never return. *Does he want me closer to his family? If so, why?*

"Now, about those books." Hamilton must stretch because I hear a satisfied groan escape him. It causes my belly to flutter as I imagine him without a shirt, his abs on display. "From what you've shared in the past, Cameron is accomplished—she's well known in the publishing community. If she feels your books are good, they must be. You need to believe her."

"Once the shock wore off, I did believe her. She both flattered and scared me. I had only thought of publishing once or twice and never looked into it. I had too many other things in my life that needed my attention. Now that she opened my mind to the possibility, I want it. I want it bad." I close my eyes for a moment. I Imagine my books on a library shelf, on a bookstore shelf, and in a school library.

"When is her pitch meeting?"

"The second week of December," I inform him.

"Wow, this could happen fast then."

We continue to talk about finding out by December 14th if they want to pick me up as a new author, about the meetings with me that might follow, and how this might all occur before Christmas.

Next our conversation moves to Latham and Salem's wedding. Hamilton will be in Athens visiting his mother and sister, so he will be at the wedding. At least I know ahead of time, so I can prepare for this encounter. I briefly flash back to my shock and reaction at seeing him at Adrian and Winston's wedding last spring.

We chat about how our group of nine have changed so much from high school graduation. Two couples are already married, and both are expecting a baby. Another couple will marry in December. Little does he know two members of our group already have a daughter.

Our yawns grow more frequent. We decide I am now ready to fall asleep and say good night. Our conversation did the trick—I immediately fall asleep to dreams of Hamilton and I together raising our daughter Liberty.

31

MADISON

My December calendar grows fuller each day. Yesterday was my last day in my student-teaching placement. With my mentor's approval, I planned fun educational games to play with cheap pencils, erasers, and candy for rewards—the students loved it. I left the building at the end of the day with an armload of gifts and cards. The math teacher, social studies teacher, and administrator I worked closely with surprised me by each handing me a reference letter to use as I apply for positions. It was both a sad and exciting end to my college studies. My graduation the fifteenth is quickly approaching.

This morning, I received a call for an interview on December 17th for a long-term substitute teacher position open in January. I'm glad my many resume and application submissions are starting to reap interviews just as Hamilton predicted. My goal is for a teaching position instead of that of a temporary substitute. Alma and I celebrated my first interview call by taking Liberty out to lunch with us.

Back home now, Liberty crawls across the living room, clutches tightly to the legs of my yoga pants, and pulls herself up to stand in front of me. "Ma-ma-ma-ma-ma," she greets.

"Hey, baby girl." I close then set my laptop aside before lifting her into my lap.

"Me-me-me," she babbles as slobber escapes both corners of her mouth.

She calls me ma-ma, Alma is la-la, and McGee is me-me. At nine months, she's really starting to express herself and navigate into all sorts of places she shouldn't. As Christmas draws near, I am anxious to see her imitate Alma's grandchildren in opening gifts and playing with new toys. It should be a fun Christmas followed by her approaching first birthday.

"McGee is outside going potty," I reply to her inquiry of where her friend me-me is. "Want to go let him in?" Liberty lifts her arms signaling she wants to go. When we enter the kitchen, she calls me-me as we approach the backdoor. McGee raises his head from his large bone in the middle of the yard when we open the door. Libby again babbles me-me, and her friend runs toward us.

I kneel once we close the door to offer McGee some love. Still calling his name, Libby pats both hands upon me-me's back. I sit her on the tile floor while I grab a treat from the pantry. Aware of what I have, McGee sits a few feet from Liberty. I pry Libby's fingers open and lay the small treat in her palm. I help her extend her open hand. McGee ever patient remains seated.

"McGee come," I firmly state. He slowly approaches and careful not to hurt Liberty, takes the treat.

Libby squeals with glee and her legs flail on the tile floor. She loves licks from her puppy. We recently began assisting Liberty in sharing treats. Both Libby and McGee love this new trick. I decide to repeat it and set up my phone camera on a nearby chair to record it this time. McGee only gets one treat when he comes in. His ears perk up and he resumes a sitting position at the sound of me in his treat jar. Liberty opens her hand on her own this time. I still assist in extending the treat and I tell McGee to come. Liberty squeals before McGee even snags the treat this time.

I probably record too many common everyday items in my attempt to compile a video journal for Hamilton. In my keeping him from this part of Liberty's life, I attempt to record everything I can. Last week I purchased an external hard-drive and moved my video journal files onto it. I past the free space in the cloud I used in November. I don't want to risk my laptop as the only location of these important clips. Between the cloud and Dropbox, I have one copy saved online and now a hard-drive for another copy that I can pass along to Hamilton this off-season.

The only week Hamilton and I have free in December is the week before the wedding and now I have an interview that Monday in Columbia. I'm supposed to be in Athens that Friday for the bachelorette party. That gives me Tuesday-Thursday to tell him everything. Alma and I discussed it today. I now worry if his reaction is not as I hope, we might ruin the wedding weekend for our friends. I'm trying to decide if this is just another excuse I am creating to keep from having this difficult conversation with Hamilton or if I should wait until after the wedding.

I sit Liberty in her highchair, placing a small handful of her favorite cereal on her tray. Glancing at the wall clock, I note Alma should be home from her hair appointment soon. My cell phone rings in the living room. I ensure Libby is buckled safely in her seat before I quickly fetch the ringing phone and return to the kitchen. McGee lies protectively on the floor near the high chair.

I quickly listen to the voicemail message from an unknown number. It's Cameron calling from her work line, so I redial.

"Hi there," she greets. "Have a minute to chat?"

"Yep, sorry I didn't answer. I had to make sure Liberty was safe in the high chair, your mom is at the salon, and my cell phone was in the living room." I'm out of breath.

"I pitched your two books this morning," Cameron begins. Her pause worries me. "D.C. Bland Publishing will be contacting you in the next 24 hours to let you know they want you as their new author-of-the-year. This is our parent company—that's the big publishing house. They only take on one new author per year and they've chosen you."

My head spins. "Seriously?"

"I told you to be ready," she proudly reminds me of our Thanks-giving discussion. "When they call they will set up meetings and travel for you to Dallas so be ready for that."

"You just pitched, and they said yes?"

"No, they received a copy of the manuscripts two days ago. Several staff members read, take notes, and pass them to the next person. So, when I pitched at the meeting, they were already in love with your stories." Cameron speaks to someone on her end before returning to our phone conversation. "When I began my pitch, they interrupted asking for more information about you, the author, and not the stories they already loved. I told them you lived with my mother, were soon to graduate from the University of Missouri with a degree in education, were from the small town of Athens, MO, and were only twenty-years-old. I figure anything else is your story to tell."

"They asked to see your manuscript with my first edit notes. They were extremely impressed with the level of writing prior to the first edit. Honey, they are in love with your work. Prepare for much flattery when they contact and meet with you." I can hear Cameron sip from a beverage. "And best of all, they've appointed me as your editor. This means I will be at all meetings and we will get to work closely together. I can even have Bland Publishing pay for my trips to see you at mom's. How cool is that?"

I think Cameron is more excited than I am. In my wildest imagi-nation I didn't see this coming, even with Cameron telling me it prob-ably would. We chat for a bit and she makes me promise to call her once they officially call me.

I sit stunned at the kitchen table when Alma returns home. McGee barks and runs to the front door to greet her. I am just coming out of my trance when she enters the kitchen.

"La-la-la," Liberty greets Alma.

Alma looks at me concerned. I fill her in on the call I just received from Cameron. As her excitement builds, my shock wears off, and the reality of the information Cameron shared begins to set in.

32

MADISON

I lay my cell phone on the coffee table while Alma's bugged-out eyes stare at me for information. "I am flying to Dallas December 19-20th." I can't form any other words.

"Let me fetch my calendar. We have a busy week that week." I love the fact her cell phone and laptop have digital calendars, yet she still prefers a paper calendar posted on the kitchen wall to schedule all of her events. When she returns with a pencil in hand we discuss the rest of December. I graduate on the 15th, our all-church Bible study potluck is the 16th, I have an interview on the 17th, will be in Dallas the 19-20th, have a bachelorette party the 21st in Athens, and then Salem's wedding on the 22nd. She mentions her family will arrive the 23rd as I return from Athens.

"I think it is best if I stay here with Liberty while you head to Dallas. We can prepare for the holiday company and you can focus on your meetings."

I agree with her and thank her once again for all she does for Liberty and me. She suggests I call my friends and Hamilton to share my news. I don't have the energy to fill the girls in, so I text to see if Hamilton is free.

Me: text /call when u have few minutes to chat

An hour later, Hamilton's video call rings my cell phone. I quickly signal from Alma to Liberty before heading for my bedroom.

"I assume you've heard something since you asked me to call." Hamilton's deep voice greets and every cell in my body stands at attention.

"Can't a fan just need to speak to her sports hero?" I tease.

"C'mon, I'm dying here. Share please." He sounds frustrated and desperate.

I share in great detail the call from D.C. Bland Publishing. I explain I am now flying to Dallas for two days and can't come to Athens early as we had discussed. He promises we will find time to visit after the holidays and before he heads to spring training in Mesa, AZ. Seems I've found yet another reason to avoid introducing Liberty to her father. I worry the longer I put it off, the worse it will be when I do.

Hamilton catches me off guard when he claims if he didn't have a meeting with PepsiCo, he'd fly to Dallas with me. *Is that something he'd do as a friend?* Maybe if we both lived in Athens he would accompany me as a friend, but he's in Chicago and I'm in Columbia. Maybe I am just wishful thinking that it means more than it does. I'm still hopeful. I'm not sure when I will get the opportunity to confess, but I am growing more and more hopeful that he is more understanding and happier than mad at me.

Holding my sleepy girl, I smile while wishing Alma a good night. She inquires the reason for my smile. I confess I've filled another spiral notebook. I'm such a nerd—I'm excited to write in a new notebook tonight. It's a blank slate and I'm giddy to create a new story on its pages. I take pride in the knowledge it's my tenth notebook—I'll need to buy several more soon.

33

MADISON

My college graduation is finally here. I can't describe the relief I feel that my hard work is over. I'm graduating two years earlier than my peers. Now, I need to find a district that will hire a twenty-year-old college graduate.

I gaze at the reflection in my full-length mirror. Alma took me shopping this week for a new dress. Of course, I protested claiming I wanted to just wear slacks and a blouse from my closet. Alma had none of that, insisting a big event requires a new dress. Ever the shopper, she dragged me to five stores before we found anything she loved. I'm not one to stand out, to wear daring or eye-catching attire that draws attention to myself. I didn't like the dress when she tossed it over the changing room door at me. I reluctantly slipped it on and immediately knew we had found my dress.

The red dress resembles the famous Marilyn Monroe white halter dress. It's snug to the waist and free-flowing from the hips to the knee. The crimson color is perfect for the holiday season and any special occasions the rest of the year. As graduation is inside and I'll wear a gold gown over it, Alma claims I will only need a cardigan to wear after the ceremony at the reception. We found sexy red heels and a matching cardigan at the same store.

Alma wraps on my open bedroom door. "There's mama," she attempts to calm Liberty.

Alma's daughters Taylor and Cameron along with Taylor's two daughters, flew in last night to surprise me for my graduation. They claimed it is a known fact that sisters must attend a baby sister's college graduation. I fear I might never get used to this large family atmosphere. Liberty has been going one-hundred miles an hour since she woke at seven this morning. She is in desperate need of a nap. I hope she falls asleep in the car and naps most of the ceremony. I'm hoping since the December graduation isn't as long as the spring ceremony, she won't need to leave the auditorium during the ceremony

"Why don't you pull a t-shirt on before you hold her. We don't want drool or spit-up to ruin such a beautiful dress." Alma never ceases to amaze me with her knowledge on all things.

With t-shirt on, I pull Liberty toward my chest and shoulder. She places an open-mouth drool-soaked kiss upon my chin before resting her head on my shoulder. I ask Alma to grab my heels and sweater from my bed as we head downstairs to join the others. Taylor offers to drive her rented mini-van and we all pile inside. Liberty is asleep before the end of the block—I breathe a sigh of relief. I want my daughter at my graduation. We've been through so much this year and I want to be able to tell her stories of attending my graduation as she grows up. I've worried since she missed her nap at eleven this morning, she might cry, causing someone to leave the auditorium and miss my ceremony with her. I can't seem to stop worrying.

Taylor looks to her daughters through the rearview mirror to the third-row seats. "Trenton, Cameron, and I all graduated from Mizzou."

"Do we have to go to Missouri?" They ask apparently thinking it is not something they want to do.

Taylor informs them they are free to choose the college best for them. She's just proud that I am following in my adopted-siblings' footsteps. It warms my heart that Liberty and I are welcome in this family.

One graduate stands between me and my diploma. I am nervous to walk up the steps and across the stage in my heels. I wish I hadn't let Alma insist I choose them over flats. At my turn I climb the four steps as my name is announced. I pose for my photo diploma in hand. I can hear raucous cheers from my family and church friends. A deep male voice catches my attention. I quirk my head while exiting the stage to hear better.

Hamilton is here? Hamilton is here! He told me he had meetings this weekend and heads to Athens on Monday. He lied. *Crap!* If he is with Alma's family, he will see Liberty. My heartrate quickens. With her dark curls, brown eyes, and his smile there is no way he won't find Liberty's resemblance to him interesting. As I attempt not to fall down the steps to resume my seat, I chant *'please don't let him see Alma.'* This week is too important and too busy to add the baby-daddy discussion with Hamilton to it. My ears ring and my head throbs as the ceremony drones on.

After the ceremony, I frantically scan the crowd as I wait for my row to be dismissed. My heart pounds against my chest wall. My ears still ring and I'm sweating. Finally, in the distant hallway, I see Alma in our pre-determined spot. I notice Cameron holding a still sleeping Liberty in her arms. I quickly scan the area unable to see Hamilton with Alma's family and my church friends. Perhaps I imagined his voice cheering for me earlier. A tap on my shoulder causes me to jump.

"Congratulations," Hamilton murmurs from behind me. I nervously turn to face him. He wraps me in a tight embrace whispering in my ear. "I knew you would do it. A college grad at age twenty." He slowly releases his hug, while keeping his hands on my forearms.

"Thank you," I whisper. My voice sounds weak. I fear he's seen Liberty with Alma. "I thought you had meetings this weekend." I worry what his next words might be.

"I couldn't ruin my surprise. You didn't think your number one fan would skip your graduation, did you?"

I smile up at him while inside I tremble like a Chihuahua.

"I can't stay long, I promised mom I'd be in Athens for dinner with pictures of you on your big day. She planned to attend with me, but she caught a terrible cold. She didn't want to be coughing loudly annoying the other proud parents at the ceremony." I can only nod at his words. *Memphis planned to attend my graduation? My own mother didn't attend my high school or college graduation.*

"Can we ask someone to snap a picture of us before I head out?" He looks in the nearby crowd.

Alma approaches and offers to take the picture after Hamilton hugs her and asks the favor. He pulls me tight to his side. His hot body and hands spark life to all parts of me. I hope I smiled in the photos Alma took. I'm not really in control at the moment. Alma points out her family to Hamilton and he waves at all the girls. I am thankful Taylor and Cameron keep Liberty at a distance and only wave back.

Alma gives us some space as Hamilton pulls me tight. He leans down to my temple placing a kiss then whispering, "I am so proud of you. I can't wait to see you at Latham's wedding this weekend. I love you." Another kiss is placed upon my temple before he pulls away waving before disappearing into the crowd.

I blink rapidly. *Did that really happen, or did I just imagine Hamilton was here?* My body is still hot where his hands and lips made contact. My blood hums through my veins. I'm grateful he attended but a few minutes are nowhere near long enough in his presence. I can't prevent the wave of feelings that flood my system. Excitement, happiness, lust, love, anxiety, fear, and dread hit all at once. It's more than I can take.

Alma slips a tissue into my hand before squeezing me tightly to her side. "You'll be okay." I nod. "Blot your eyes. The girls are anxiously waiting to see you."

I dab tears from the corner of each eye with shaking hands. Alma hugs me and whispers he didn't see Liberty, but it was a close call.

She tells me this is not the time to dwell on it, we need to celebrate. Taylor and Cameron give me knowing smiles before joining Taylor's daughters. The noise wakes Liberty and she immediately stretches her arms to me.

Alma and Taylor snap several photos of us all before asking a gentleman nearby to take a few of our entire group. I'm on autopilot. My mind on Hamilton, I pose and attempt to smile when prompted. Taylor offers to take everyone to CC's City Broilers claiming she has a reservation. I am not in the mood to celebrate—Hamilton's attendance zapped everything from me, but I still find the energy to pretend for my family.

This is my first visit to CC's, I've heard Alma and many from church share about the divine meals they've enjoyed here. Cameron shares that their father insisted on dinner at CC's for birthdays and graduations. It humbles me that they include me in yet another tradition. My eyes are the size of saucers when I notice the prices on the menu. Taylor leans my way whispering her husband insisted they treat me to dinner here in exchange for my sharing an experience at Wrigley and meeting Hamilton with them while in Chicago a year ago. I'm cognizant of the fact that I paid nothing at Wrigley when I arranged to meet Hamilton. Taylor and her husband paid for the tickets and are now paying for this meal.

I order the lobster tail and petite filet with asparagus. On a trip to Kansas City once in high school, Adrian, Salem, Savannah, Bethany, and I splurged to eat at Red Lobster. We each ordered different items, so we could taste them all. Surprisingly I loved everything. This is definitely not a Red Lobster. I'm sure this meal will be among the best I've ever ordered. Taylor orders a bottle of wine for the table and sparkling water for her daughters. Before our meal arrives, they toast my graduation, upcoming job interview, and upcoming meetings in Dallas.

34

MADISON

As the approaching holidays and Salem's wedding draw near, I receive more texts from the girls in Athens. Alma's daughters and the girls left shortly after noon today. Alma is giving Libby a bath in the kitchen sink while I read the texts bombarding my phone this evening. The girls must have planned to all text me at seven.

Adrian: I'm officially 6 months pregnant!
Adrian: I have trouble sleeping & I'm always horny
Adrian: of course Winston doesn't mind that part
Me: TMI

I quickly interrupt while trying to keep the images from forming in my mind. That's way too much information.

Bethany: I'm 2 months pregnant!

Bethany: I told Troy last night
Bethany: He's freaked out & going to be over-the-top protective

I imagine Adrian and Bethany's kids growing up together. Bethany & I know my daughter is the oldest child in our little group. I find I long more and more each day to share my secret with the rest of these ladies.

Bethany: Troy's 20th birthday weekend of wedding
Bethany: is accepted to the academy in St. Joe
Bethany: starts cop school this summer
Me: (I text a pic of my college diploma)

It suddenly feels like bragging—I hadn't thought about that. Adrian chose to open her resale shop and not attend college. Bethany attended Athens Community College for a year before dropping out to provide childcare and become a mother. Salem attended a one-year LPN program at the community college and now works at the hospital. And Savannah works full-time as a bakery manager at the grocery store. I'm the only one to achieve my degree, but I'm glad they are all happy on their own paths.

Me: now for biggest news
Adrian: if u hooked up with Hamilton & didn't call
Adrian: I'm gonna be pissed @ u
Savannah: what's big news?
Me: publishing house in Dallas is flying me down
Me: Dec. 19th & 20th to discuss publishing 2 of my (book emoji)
Bethany: What books?

Salem: (book emoji)?

Of my group of friends in Athens, Savannah and Adrian knew of my previous writings. While they never read any of them, I did share that I wrote stories in my spare time while hiding in my bedroom at home.

Salem: what type of books are they?
Me: young adult
Me: some middle school & others high school age
Adrian: did u write about any of us?

I regret mentioning anything during their texts. It would have been easier to chat at the upcoming wedding or not to tell them at all. I've opened this can of worms, so I have to continue.

Me: aren't based on any 1 real-life
Me: characters have pieces of us
Me: aren't entirely like any 1 of us
Me: no need to worry

After congratulating me and wishing me luck on my trip to Dallas, Salem texts to remind us we have five days until her bachelorette party and six days until her wedding. The girls text excitedly for a few minutes about all of the details, when I will arrive, and the honeymoon.

Last but not least, Savannah texts that the bakery is incredibly busy for the holidays. She is taking Friday and Saturday off for Salem's wedding, so she won't fall asleep standing up at Salem's events. She hasn't had a day off since the second week of November and she can't wait for January when everything slows down again.

As we end our text session, my friends wish me good luck at my meetings in Dallas on Wednesday and Thursday.

Alma carries Libby bundled snuggly in her towel towards me. My tired girl smiles at me.

"Are you ready for bed?" I ask as I sweep her into my arms towel and all.

"She almost fell asleep in the sink," Alma claims.

As I secure a diaper on my wiggling daughter she giggles. I wonder if Alma imagined Liberty's sleepiness as she is very active now. In her sleeper, we begin to rock in the corner of her room. I tell her all about our busy week ahead.

"Da-da-da," my beautiful girl asks me. With baseball games almost daily for months, she's now gone quite a while without us pointing out or talking about Hamilton on TV.

I tell her daddy is in Athens. I realize she doesn't understand me, so I pull my cell phone from my back pocket and display the photo of Hamilton and I at my graduation. I point to Hamilton, "Daddy."

Liberty attempts to pull the phone from my hands. When that doesn't work, she points. As she points I say daddy or mommy depending on who she points to.

At this moment tears form in my eyes. I've let her down as a parent. I've kept her daddy away from her for much too long. Hamilton will be a perfect father and Liberty deserves to know him. I must find a time in January to talk to him about her. I can't let another off-season pass and keep my secret. I hand Libby her bottle and lay my phone on a nearby table.

As my daughter quickly slides to sleep, I imagine my conversation with Hamilton revealing Liberty as his daughter. As I have hundreds of times before, I attempt to think of all possible outcomes, the perfect location, and the perfect words to use.

35

MADISON

When I return home Monday, I check on Liberty napping in her crib before I change from my interview suit. I barely have my yoga pants on when Bethany pops on the screen of my ringing phone. I answer the video call.

"So, how did the interview go?" Bethany immediately asks, making it clear her reason for calling me.

As I hang my suit in the closet and return my heels to the shelf I answer. "They hired me on the spot. I start on January Fourth. I'll be teaching social studies and current events at the middle school for at least five weeks."

Bethany smiles and claps the entire time I talk. She asks if she can tell the others in Athens and I give her permission. I am much too busy this week to worry about another long phone call to the girls.

"What does Libby think of her mommy's new job?" Bethany segues to her favorite part of our private video calls.

I walk into the nursery with the camera facing away from me. Although she was sound asleep only moments ago, she's standing at the railing of her crib smiling when I enter.

"There's my girl," Bethany announces through the phone. "Hi, Libby."

I lean my phone with the camera pointed at Libby's face against the wall, while I change her diaper on the changing table. Bethany coos and babbles, but Libby looks at me. As soon as my hands are free, I position the phone, so Bethany can see my daughter again.

The two jibber and jabber for long minutes before Bethany claims she hears the garage door and needs to go before Troy walks in. I tell her I'll see her Friday and we end the call.

―――――

As I wrap Liberty's Christmas gifts 'from Hamilton', I fight tears while I imagine her big, strong father excitedly shopping then gift-wrapping them himself. Remembering the gifts he gave me during my scavenger hunt the day he left Athens, I know what a great gift-giver as a dad he will be. I know my wrapping gifts from her dad will never make up for really having Hamilton in her life. This is another reason I must introduce the two before she gets any older.

I hurry to wrap the remaining gifts as I attempt not to think of Hamilton, his future relationship with Liberty, and my failures as her mother for keeping her a secret from her dad and his family. I climb into bed knowing I will struggle with sleep as the thoughts still swarm my head.

When sleep finally comes to me it's fitful with nightmares of losing Alma. Recently my fears of Alma's age and health infiltrate my dreams in horrible scenarios. Images from these nightmares haunt me when I should enjoy my time with her. I over analyze every ache she mentions, and her occasional memory lapses.

―――――

Friday arrives before I know it. I enjoy a slow easy breakfast with Liberty in her chair near me. When I arrived home last night she was already in bed for the night. I spent Wednesday and Thursday away from her and today I will leave for two days in Athens while she stays home again with Alma. Every day away from her seems like an eternity. I want to help my friends celebrate, but the thought of leaving my precious girl in an hour sickens me. I need to finally confess to Hamilton, so I'll no longer have to travel without her.

Alma allows me time alone with my daughter before offering to help me load my car for my next journey. I've only packed a small suitcase and a garment bag—Alma carries them to the car while I soak up another hug and smother Liberty with kisses. I've learned fast goodbyes are best and am soon on my way to Athens.

36

MADISON

Bluetooth interrupts my playlist over the speakers to announce I have a call just as I pull into the city limits of Athens.

"I just pulled into town," I inform Hamilton instead of saying hello.

"Good, I was worried."

"Why?"

He explains I mentioned the time I planned to leave Columbia and with that I should have arrived an hour ago. I can't admit that I needed one more hour with Liberty before I left on yet another trip. Instead I promise that my reason for running late is a great one that I will share over lunch with them in about twenty minutes as I am stopping for gas on my way through town. I've been busy this week—I still need to tell him all of my good news.

Before I park my car, Memphis and Hamilton walk my way. Hamilton opens my door for me. Memphis wraps me in a tight hug and Hamilton joins us.

"Guys, I can't breathe," I sputter.

They release me, help me with my bags, and lead me into the house. Just as I thought she would, Memphis has lunch ready for us.

Hamilton whisks my items upstairs while Memphis orders me to take a seat. I don't dare disobey her. When Hamilton returns we eat.

"Spill it," Hamilton orders.

Memphis swats his right arm. "Hamilton Armstrong, where are your manners? I raised you better than that."

Smiling sugary sweet, Hamilton looks from his mother to me. "Madison, sweetheart, please share with the two of us about your interview on Monday and your trip to Dallas." Hamilton lays his politeness on very thick—I can only laugh. Memphis rolls her eyes at me. I've missed the two of them.

"The middle school hired me on the spot Monday. I start January 4th for at least five weeks teaching social studies." I smile at Memphis before taking a few more bites.

I didn't anticipate Hamilton's reaction. He runs over to my side of the table to hug me from behind while I remain seated. He claims we need to celebrate. I remind him we have bachelor and bachelorette parties tonight and a wedding tomorrow, we can celebrate there. Hamilton returns to his seat but doesn't resume eating. He awaits the rest of my good news. I take two more bites chewing slowly to make him wait a bit longer.

"D.C. Bland Publishing chose me as their new author of the year for the upcoming year. They plan to publish my first book by late-summer then slowly release my other books after that. Cameron will be my editor and contact person. She will get to travel to visit Alma and me on the company dime while we talk business. It all seems very surreal."

Both Memphis and Hamilton talk excitedly about this news. I try to answer questions when I can and promise to share more as I learn about it. Memphis requests to read my manuscripts prior to publication and I promise to send a digital copy to her soon.

After lunch we remain at the kitchen table to catch up on Hamilton's many endorsement deals and public appearances past and future. I feel at ease and comfortable at the Armstrong table. I wonder when I divulge my secret about Liberty if I will still be welcome and comfortable. If I am not, I pray Liberty will be.

Hamilton invites me to help him make a few repairs outside, but I opt to visit with Memphis this afternoon claiming I need to rest for tonight and tomorrow's activities after my travels to Dallas and drive to Athens this morning.

Memphis and I visit for a bit then quietly read while Hamilton busies himself outside. I'm half sitting half lying on the sofa while I read on my Kindle App. Memphis rocks as she reads her book.

"I hope the two of you will find some time this afternoon or tomorrow to talk." Memphis closes her book in her lap. I look up from my phone. "I'm a mom and a mom can sense when there is something up. The two of you..." She tucks hair behind her right ear. "I've tried not to interfere, but it's been a year."

She moves close beside me on the sofa. Holding my hand in hers she informs me she knows I'm hiding something. "It's more than just moving away to college. During your video calls and even now, your eyes give you away. I can tell you are happy to be here, but there is something you are holding back." She raises her palm out to me when I begin to speak. "Now, I won't push—it's your life. I just want you to know I am here for you. You can tell me anything—I'm here to help in any way I can. If you just need a shoulder to cry on or an ear to listen, I'm here for that, too. If you can't talk to me, I want to encourage you to talk to Hamilton. I realize he is very busy and usually so far away, but he's here today and tomorrow for you. He'll be here until after Christmas. I just hate seeing you hold back."

She takes a deep breath. "The same goes for him. Something is up. I don't know if it is stress, his team, his appearances, or what. I've tried a few times to get him to open up with no luck." She shakes her head then stands frustrated. "I feel helpless. I can see the two of you suffering a bit, but I can't fix it if I'm not let in."

Before she leaves the room, I call to her. "Memphis, you're right. I do have something I just can't share it yet. I'm still trying to work a few things out. I've almost called you a hundred times but am not ready quite yet." I take her hand in mine. "I know you are here for me. I need to share this with him first and it's never been the right time."

"It will never be the *perfect* time. Life is unpredictable. You need to get it off your chest before it festers too big to do anything about. I assume by him you mean my son." I nod. "Hamilton loves you—talk to him. It's the off-season. He has a while before he reports to spring training. Take a deep breath and then tell him whatever it is. You'll feel better just getting it off your chest."

I nod and return to the sofa. I don't open my phone. I can't read now. I should have known I couldn't hide from Memphis. I want to tell her. I could do it right now then ask her how to break the news to her son. In my heart I am ready for everyone to know, but I can't take the spotlight off Salem and Latham's wedding. I can't do it with Liberty so far away—they will want to see her immediately.

Again, it's not the right time.

Memphis kindly gives me time to myself. She mentioned Hamilton is keeping something from her, too. I wonder if it might be about me. It could be work and his busy off-season schedule this year. I'm sure he knows he can talk to me if he needs to. I don't want to push it, though. As much as I want to know if his constantly touching and kissing me means something, I'm not ready for that discussion either. I close my eyes deciding to focus on Salem and her wedding activities. The rest will work itself out in time.

37

HAMILTON

As I walk back toward the barn, I remember anxiously awaiting Madison's arrival this morning. I wish I could turn back time. I'd sweep her into the barn immediately when she arrived. I'd kiss her breathless and while she caught her breath I'd spill my heart to her. I'd tell her I love her, I'd tell her I want her in my life every day, and I'd ask her to consider moving our relationship forward.

When she began to argue, I'd share I imagine us married, starting a family, and living in Chicago year-round. In my dreams, she teaches in Chicago, she's actively involved in the middle school, and often shares stories from school at our dinner table. I'd explain my strong desire to ask her to marry me, but realize we need to date, to solve our long-distance issues, and reconnect first.

I climb on the four-wheeler and peel out of the barn much too fast seeking the open pasture. As I drive my heart aches at her excitement of her new temporary teaching position. In my ear I hear mom saying, 'if you snooze you lose'. Because I hesitated in sharing my feelings, I can no longer share as it will make her choose career or me.

The excitement on her face and in her voice as she shared about her temporary job, I can't ask her to give that up to be with me. I want her near me and I want her happy. I know how hard she worked in high school, throughout the past year to earn her degree, and to secure this job. I can't cause her to lose that light in her eyes. I can't ask her to choose me over the temporary position.

I'm such an idiot. I'm out here zooming around on an ATV that my coach and agent would have a coronary if they knew about when I want to be with Madison. My goal is to spend as much time with her this weekend as I can. It's time to stop pouting, man up, and enjoy the weekend with Madison while I can be near her.

38

MADISON

The day passes quickly, before I know it, Hamilton drops me off at Adrian's house for Salem's bachelorette party. Tonight's festivities will be the exact opposite of the crazy event I planned for Adrian's bachelorette party.

"Uh-huh," Adrian shakes her head, placing a hand on Hamilton's chest. "This is a bachelorette party; no guys allowed. You just hop back in your truck and drive your butt over to Troy's."

Hamilton grabs my elbow preventing me from entering the house. "Call me when you are ready for a ride home. I'll be here in five minutes," he whispers in my ear before he places a soft kiss at the corner of my lips then returns to his truck.

I stand on Adrian's porch waving as he backs from the driveway. His husky whisper ignited tiny fires throughout my body. My lips burn where his perfectly plump hot lips left his kiss. Adrian is mumbling something from the doorway behind me. I can't quite make out her words, but it sounds like such a cute couple. When I can no longer watch Hamilton, I'm ready to focus on the girls and start our party.

"You're the first to arrive," Adrian states with a giant smile on her face. As she hangs my coat in the entryway closet, she states drinks and snacks are in the kitchen. "So, Hamilton and you are staying with Memphis this weekend, how cozy." She waggles her eyebrows up and down.

"Stop it," I warn. "It's not like that and you know it. Nothing has changed. I'm just as confused now as I was months ago. I'm going along with the feelings he demonstrates. Seems we are very friendly friends."

Adrian cocks a brow. "How do you feel about that?"

"Confused," I answer honestly with a groan. "I'm confused. We've been close since eighth grade. He's still my best friend, and I am still his number one fan. I live each day anxiously awaiting a text or phone call from him. It feels good seeing him again today. Everything is smooth like it was in high school except for a kiss to my lips or cheeks from time to time. The kisses seem friendly, I assume that's what we are, just friends." I shrug and snag a diet cola from the fridge.

Bethany and Salem barge through the unlocked front door without knocking, announcing Savannah just pulled into the driveway. With the gang all here, it's time to start the party. Once we all gather around the kitchen island, Bethany shares the party plans.

"Ladies," Bethany raises her voice to get everyone's attention. "Tonight, we are keeping it simple. All drinks are non-alcoholic in honor of us two pregnant women. We will eat, visit, play games, watch movies, and snack. Nothing too wild as requested by our bride-to-be Salem." She motions toward our friend.

"Sounds great," Salem announces. "Bring on the food."

Adrian pulls deli trays from the refrigerator and I place the buns and condiments for sandwiches nearby. We open several bags of chips and two tubs of dip, then dig in. We choose to visit then watch the latest romantic comedy release. I enjoy every minute with my girls. I don't pretend here—they take me as I am. Although we talk almost weekly, I find there is still so much I miss out on.

"Things must be very different for you in Columbia."

I meet Salem's eyes before I answer. "Yeah, my life is very differ-

ent. I haven't needed to use Tater Hill, Wilson Holler, or Coon Creek
(*pronounced krik*) to give directions in over a year." I tease my friends.

"We know," Adrian chides. "you love it in the big city and don't
miss Athens-life."

I don't correct my friend. I don't confide in my girls that I miss
them and Athens. I can't tell them I long to raise Liberty in this small
town. I don't share in my year away I've come to realize my distaste
for Athens had much more to do with my mother and not small-town
life as I believed.

An hour and a half later, Bethany starts our movie and we settle in
with snacks on our laps. We chat and laugh the entire movie. I notice
Salem keeps texting someone and looks concerned by the latest
message.

"Everything okay?" I whisper, not wanting to draw everyone's
attention to her.

"My mom says the boiler at the church isn't working. She's on her
way to the church to meet a repairman. It's too cold to hold the
wedding tomorrow without heat." Concern is written all over her
face.

"Adrian is asleep, and Bethany looks ready to doze off at any
time." I point in their direction. Savannah listens in on our conversation now. "We could call it a night to let the pregnant mommies rest
and you can join them at the church."

Salem hesitates, but I decide to end the party for her. "Ladies, I
think it's time to clean up the kitchen and let our future mommies get
some sleep." Adrian's eyes snap open and we make quick work of the
clean-up.

39

MADISON

I pull out my cell phone to call Hamilton for a ride as we planned.

"Mady!" Hamilton yells in greeting. Without pulling the receiver from his mouth he slurs to the men. "Guys, she's on the phone. Stop. Stop. Troy it's your turn." I can't make out Troy's words. "Bull shit!" Hamilton yells. "I call bull shit!"

Sensing something is up, I signal for the ladies to be quiet by putting my index finger over my lips and set my phone to speaker. The girls gather around to hear better.

"Hamilton, you suck!" Troy yells.

"Shut up and chug," Latham slurs loudly.

"Drink. Drink. Drink." The men chant for Troy.

Next, we hear Hamilton say, "Two fours."

Then Troy yells, "Bull shit."

Hamilton attempts to taunt while slurring, "Are you sure Troy, you'll have to drink if you're wrong."

"I call bull shit!" Troy reiterates.

Hamilton groans then seems to chug a drink while the other three chant. The ladies begin to giggle around me. We haven't heard Winston, but it sounds like the other guys are drunk.

"Hamilton," I call with a raised voice. We hear the game continue as if I am not on his phone. "Hamilton!" Still nothing from his end, so I hang up.

"Can someone give me a ride over to Troy and Bethany's house? I think I need to drive Hamilton home tonight."

Savannah offers to drive me, but Bethany chimes in. "Why don't the three of you ride with me? I bet Adrian will need to drive Winston and Salem you'll need to drive Latham. If I take you, then you'll only have your guy's car to drive." It makes perfect sense. We say our good-byes to Savannah with promises to see her at the wedding before we pile into Bethany's minivan for the short drive to her house.

Although the phone call led us to believe all four guys were drunk, we were not prepared for the mess and how drunk they all are. Upon opening the door, the strong stench of beer greets us. Bethany's morning sickness hits—she darts to the bathroom with her hand over her mouth.

We watch from the doorway for a moment as they continue their game totally unaware we stand nearby. Winston sits with a stiff back as his head wobbles from side to side and he attempts to focus on his cards. I've never witnessed Winston and Hamilton in this state of inebriation. Troy and Latham often let go on the weekends, but the other two usually only enjoy a beer or two. Latham leans his head on his hand with his elbow on the table. He struggles to keep his eyes open. While his cards lie on the table face-up in front of him for everyone to see.

We are standing behind Troy, but from his raised voice, animated actions, and mispronunciation of several words, it is clear he is drunk. Hamilton attempts to focus on the game and doesn't see us watching straight across from him.

"Hey guys," I greet.

"Hamilton look, Madison is here!" Latham yells in his drunken state.

Hamilton looks at me, then picks up his cell phone. "Madison are you still there?"

I decide to play along by walking behind his chair. "Hi, Hamilton." I pretend to still be on his phone.

"Did you need something?"

I roll my eyes towards Adrian. "Hamilton can you come pick me up? Our party is over."

"Sure," he lays his phone on the corner of the table. "Guys I gotta go. Madison needs a ride." Laughter erupts. Hamilton rises from his chair and trips over its leg. I grab his shoulders in an attempt to help him find his balance.

"Thanks Madison," he slurs.

I witness the moment he makes the connection. He looks at his phone then at me and back.

"You don't need a ride," he announces.

"No, but it seems you do," Adrian answers for me, trying to stifle her laughter.

Winston realizes they are all busted. "It's Troy's twentieth birthday so we decided to play a drinking game." He speaks to Adrian as if she is his mother and just caught him drinking.

Latham extends his arms to Salem. "We ran out of beer, so we had to use Jack Daniels." He points to the open bottle on the table.

Ah-ha that explains how lit they are. Stupid boys, I've told them several times. 'Beer before liquor never sicker. Liquor before beer in the clear.' Seems they will be bent over the toilet tonight. It amazes me in just over three hours, Hamilton and Latham forgot they needed to pick us up and drive home tonight. Winston drove himself over here, too. I'm even more glad we chose not to drink alcohol at our party tonight. Bethany and Adrian might have driven all of us home tonight if we had.

At this point we attempt to get three sets of keys from the guys. Bethany finds everyone's keys by the back door on a table and passes them to us.

I laugh so hard as I attempt to load Hamilton in his truck that I nearly pee my pants. It's like trying to help a sleepy four-year-old to bed, but he's over six-feet-tall and over two-hundred pounds. I roll his window down and encourage him to keep his nose near the fresh air as I drive. I don't want to clean up vomit from his truck tonight.

He's snoring when I park in Memphis' driveway. I shake him awake and remind him his mother is asleep, so we must be quiet on our way to his room. He tries his best to walk, but still leans heavily on my shoulders. His heavy boots bump the door frame on our way inside. I contemplate removing the boots in the mudroom or upstairs —I decide in his room will be easier. Much too loudly we make our way through the kitchen then up to his room.

He falls onto his bed placing his arm over his eyes. I shut off the overhead light and switch on the bedside lamp. *Where to begin?* I untie and slip off his heavy work boots. As I tuck them on the floor of his closet, he makes a groan before darting to the attached bathroom. I knew this would happen.

I place a wet washcloth on the back of his neck, then take a seat on the edge of the tub and rub his back while he heaves the contents of his stomach into the toilet. He's not quiet while puking. I cringe knowing Memphis surely hears him. I decide to peek into the hallway to let her know he is okay. I do not find her, and her door is still closed, so instead I fetch water and pain relievers from the kitchen.

When I return, Hamilton is sprawled out on the tile floor with the washcloth over his eyes. "Ham, I have some water if you want a sip." He groans rolls to his side and proceeds to vomit on himself and the bathroom floor. *Great, now I will get the honor of cleaning his bathroom.* I do my best to assist him toward the toilet just in time for the next round. After fifteen minutes his stomach seems to calm. With a fresh washcloth I wipe his mouth and chin.

"Ham, I need you to take a shower. You have puke all over and it might help you feel better." He doesn't respond.

I struggle to pull his t-shirt covered in puke over his head and in doing so I realize it's now in his hair. I try not to gag as I ask him to stand and remove his jeans while I turn the shower on. He struggles what seems like an eternity with his belt. It is clear I need to strip him the rest of the way. *He's sick—I can do this.* My fingers fumble nervously before successfully unhooking the belt then button on his jeans. I'm acutely aware of my knuckles brushing against his dark happy trail in the process.

My stomach somersaults as thoughts of slipping my hand further inside his jeans enter my mind. I imagine the thick, heavy weight of him in my palm, his reaction to my touch, to the movement of my hand...

"Mady, if you don't stop worrying your lip I'll have to rescue it myself," his husky whisper draws my eyes up his contoured abdominals then chest to his heavy-lidded brown eyes.

He's drunk. He's sick. Snap out of this Madison. You can't go there tonight.

Hamilton's fingers rest under my chin while his thumb pulls my lower lip away from my incisors. I wasn't aware of biting it.

"The shower is ready. Get undressed and hop in."

I sigh as he nearly falls over while attempting to remove his jeans. Placing my hands on the waistband of his pants I assist him in sliding them down his thighs. I urge him to put his hand on the wall before he steps out of each leg and his socks. I close my eyes tight as I stand back up.

"Okay, you in the shower," I order attempting to control my hormones. My body is alive. I fight the urge to press myself against him, to take him in my mouth, to seek a release for both of us. Though I try hard not to, my eyes glance down and my breath catches at the sight of his erect cock. Needing to remove myself from the room and my thoughts, I turn him toward the shower with my hands on his shoulders. I open the glass door and guide him through. When he places his two palms on the tiles under the nozzle allowing the spray to pummel his neck and back, I flee.

I squeal when Memphis scares me in the hallway on my way to my room. "Everything okay?"

I don't know if she means with me or Hamilton. "Hamilton drank too much, so I drove us home. He's been sick and now he's in the shower."

Memphis fails to hide her smile. It's clear she knows why I was darting from his bedroom. "You need anything?" When I can only shake my head, she bids me goodnight and returns to her room shutting the door behind her.

I hear the shower shut off. *Crap!* I didn't get the chance to regroup in my room. I debate turning in or checking on Hamilton one more time. I reluctantly return to assist him in finding his bed—I won't sleep until I know he is safe in his bed.

Peeking through the bathroom door. The dripping wet hunk of a man that is Hamilton Armstrong greets me. His hands are planted on the counter, a towel is secured low around his waist, and his eyes look to me in the large mirror.

"Feel better?"

He nods before squeezing toothpaste on his toothbrush then scrubbing his teeth and tongue. I lean in the door frame transfixed as his back, shoulders, and arms flex while he brushes. Hamilton clears his throat drawing my attention to his reflection. He smirks, yes, smirks at me. It seems he does feel better.

"Alright, I'm going to turn in. Please take the pain relievers and drink the entire water I put by the bed. Goodnight." I turn and head to his sister's room.

40

MADISON

I lean against the shut bedroom door allowing myself to slide to the floor. My mind still focuses on Hamilton's bare back and shoulders with water droplets glistening. His white towel secured low on his hips as it hints to what lies beneath. The eighteen months since I experienced what hid under his towel seems like only yesterday and at the same time an eternity ago.

I've replayed our time together over and over in my mind. His body, his words, and his touch are burned in my memory. Part of me desperately yearns for a repeat performance. It's been eighteen long months since I've been with him. My fantasies are no replacement for the real man only a room away.

I peel myself off the floor, slip on my pajamas, and crawl into bed. I unsuccessfully attempt to clear my mind of all things Hamilton. I flip from my back to my stomach and then from one side to the other unable to find comfort. After what seems like eons, I tiptoe to the bathroom in the hallway. I splash cool water on my face then pat it dry with the hand towel. As I return to my room, I sneak a peek into Hamilton's room to check on him.

"Hey," his sleepy voice calls as he lifts his head slightly.

"Just checking if you need anything." I twist the end of my tank-top around my finger.

"Having trouble sleeping?" When I nod, he slides over patting for me to join him. I stand frozen. "C'mon, I promise not to bite."

Hesitantly I move towards him. He lifts the covers and I slip under leaving plenty of room between our bodies. Having none of it, Hamilton wraps his arm around my waist and pulls my back snug to his front. I'm home. Wrapped in his warmth as his breathing evens out, I slide into slumber.

I fight the urge to wake as several slight tugs on my hair beckon me. Slowly I blink open my eyes adjusting to the morning light seeping in through the open blinds.

Hamilton's blinds.

Hamilton's bedroom.

The bottom falls out of my stomach at my realization I slept in his bed with his mother just down the hall.

"Good morning," Hamilton whispers from behind me. "How'd you sleep?"

His eager face shocks me. I fully expected a hungover, cranky Hamilton this morning. I planned to force a little hair of the dog down him in an attempt to help him bounce back for the wedding this afternoon.

Recalling his question, I answer. "I haven't slept this soundly in months." Guilt consumes me immediately. Being away from Liberty is equally responsible for the sound sleep as the proximity Hamilton is. I don't mind giving up sleep for her. I'd give up so much more if I needed to. She's my world and yet here I lie acting as if she doesn't exist.

"Hey," Hamilton whispers, pulling my chin towards him. He searches my eyes. "What's wrong?"

I shake my head fighting the tears that threaten. He tucks my hair behind my ear. I'm sure my bed head is atrocious. I force a smile. "How's your head?"

Hamilton assures me my nursing skills last night scared off any hangover he might have deserved. I don't believe he feels no pain, but it's clear he feels much better than he should. I decide to remedy this.

"I washed your clothes and cleaned your bathroom last night, but I couldn't bare cleaning the cab of your truck in the cold and dark." I squeeze my tongue between my teeth on the verge of hurting to fend off a smile.

A long groan rises from Hamilton's chest.

"I'm sorry, I know I should have taken care of it immediately..."

"No, it's not your fault. You cleaned much more than you should have. I shouldn't have put you in such a position." He slides from his side of the bed.

He's fully dressed. Come to think of it I smelled toothpaste while he was next to me. "How long have you been awake?"

He sits on the bed beside me. He's been up for an hour or so, he even ate breakfast and got a tongue lashing from Memphis. She ran to town for a bit, so he came to wake me up. When he excuses himself to go clean his truck, I admit I was teasing. Before I can react, he tackles me on his bed, braces my hands above my head with one of his hands, and tickles my ribs. I squirm attempting to escape. I flail desperately in my attempts to evade him.

His dark brown eyes lock on mine and we freeze. I'm extremely aware of the alignment of our pelvic regions, the fact that he pinned my hands just like this the night we were together, and we are alone in the house. Every cell springs to life—my body hums. My nipples pebble in my thin tank, it suddenly feels one-hundred degrees in his room, and I can't peel my eyes from his.

"Breathe Madison," his husky voice growls just as he did our first time together.

Slowly he closes the distance between our lips. When I can take his slow descent no more, I fight against his restraint to meet him.

"Patience," he chuckles mere inches from my mouth. "We are in no rush."

Finally, he allows his plump, warm lips to meet mine. I moan and melt under him. I part my lips granting him access to more of me. His warm tongue strokes mine, stoking fires deep inside me. Always needing more, I lift my pelvis infinitesimally to grind against his. He tugs my lower lip between his teeth pulling back slightly and I grind again. He moves, kissing behind my ear, licking, then blowing. His breath causes goosebumps on my damp skin. I tilt my head exposing more neck for his attention. My core is on fire.

"Ham," I beg.

"Yes?" He moves kissing my collarbone still pinning my hands above my head.

"Ham, I need..." He nips then kisses.

"Tell me what you *need*."

"Ham, please I need you, now, everywhere," my husky voice further demonstrates my arousal for only him.

He wastes no time. He releases my hands, pulls up my tank, and tugs off my boxer shorts. His eyes turn molten as he scans my body head to toe. I no longer have the tight body he's seen before. I have more curves at my breast and hips along with stretch marks. Suddenly I'm worried what he might find on his explorations. I throw my arms around his neck and pull his mouth to mine. My kiss is primal, needing him inside me now.

Hamilton pulls away, reaching for a condom. I tug him back.

"I'm protected and I'm clean." I stare into his eyes.

"Um," he hesitates. His eyes search mine. "I *always* wear a condom."

"I'm giving you permission to skip the condom. I get a shot every three months. I'm not going to get pregnant." *This time* I think to myself. "I've only been with you." I sound desperate as I try to talk him in to entering me.

"I'm clean." He clears his throat. "You really haven't been with anyone else?"

"Only you," I promise.

He throws my leg around his waist, gently places himself at my wet opening, then with eyes on mine slowly glides in to the root. I raise my other leg around him. As he finds a delectable rhythm, my eyes close unable to fight to keep them open any longer. My fingers dig into his shoulders and my head falls back into the mattress. Hamilton's mouth is everywhere. He kisses my lips, licks my neck, and sucks on my nipples. He slides one hand between us. At first contact I groan and grind into his fingertips. Quickly I wind tighter and tighter, growing closer to my release.

Hamilton trails kisses from my breast, to my collarbone while his stubble scrapes and ignites my sensitive skin. His hot breath fills my ear. "I'm not going to last, you feel so good around me, so hot, so..."

His words combined with his fingertips and to his thrusts are my undoing. I scream his name as my orgasm hits. I arch, I grind, I beg him not to stop. Every muscle tightens, my breath hitches and white flashes of light shoot in every direction behind my closed lids. "Y-e-s!" I growl.

Hamilton's hand on my hip bites into my flesh holding me as he pounds again and again. His other hand winds in my hair and pulls me toward his chest. With one, two, three more thrusts he shutters inside me. His veins pop out in his neck and his head looks to the ceiling. I feel his growl move from his abdomen, through his chest, and escape his open mouth.

"F-u-c-k," his breath comes in rapid pants as his every muscle relaxes over me. He falls beside me, breaking our connection.

I stare at the ceiling afraid to make eye contact with him. I really messed up. I need to tell him about his daughter before I allow myself to be confused by our relationship. As my breaths slow and my body relaxes, I worry how Hamilton will feel when he finds out I had sex with him while keeping his daughter a secret. *Why am I making things worse instead of opening up to him?*

"I haven't either," Hamilton states, turning to face me.

I struggle to understand him. *Did he speak while I was lost in my head?* I turn toward him, my brows raised.

"Since we were together, I haven't been with anyone else."

His words are a hundred-pound anvil to my chest. As if I needed anything else to complicate things, his confession is everything I want to hear. Tears pool and my throat closes tight.

"Mady, don't cry." Hamilton pulls me tight against his chest. His hands rub up and down my bare back. "Sweetheart, what's wrong?"

I shake my head. If it weren't for Salem's wedding, I could spill my guts right here, right now. I know lying naked in his arms is not how I want to share we have a daughter. I want to, I need to unburden myself of my secret. "I..." my voice quivers. I take in a deep breath then exhale. "I've got something major I'm working through. I need to plan some things out before I can share it with you." I glance into his eyes.

His brow is furrowed. "I can help you if you let me," he offers.

I have no doubt how he will help once he knows the truth. This is just not the right time. "Your mom asked me about it yesterday. I guess she can see I'm holding something back. I just can't tell the two of you, yet." His eyes beg me to open up. "I need some more time, I need to do something first, and then I promise I'll share it with you."

Internally I cringe at my words. I make my daughter sound like a burden, a complication that I am avoiding for the time being. I can't give any hints to my secret. I need to change the subject before I mess this up further.

"Your mom claims you are keeping something from us, too."

My words hang heavy in the air. He sighs heavily while scrubbing his hands over his dark stubbled face and into his hair. "I've just been so busy, it seems like I have no off-season that's all."

Although it's the truth, I know Memphis speaks of something bigger than this. I feel like a bad friend as I didn't notice until Memphis mentioned it. He does carry a burden. We used to tell each other everything. We helped each other come up with plans and ideas to solve our problems. Life was much simpler when we were in high school, visited our cemetery, and were available to each other 24/7.

Hamilton's long muscular arms wrap around me. "I hate being so far away from you most of the year. I want you with me—I need you in my life."

His confession fills me with hope and scares me to death at the same time. I can't contain the hiccuping sobs that overtake me. He kisses my forehead and nose before hugging me. One arm holds me tight against him at my shoulders, the other glides up and down my bare back.

"It's okay, we will find a way. I promise." I hear his words but continue to cry. "We will figure something out—we will find a way to make *us* work."

"You may not..." I wipe my running nose on the back of my hand and I gulp in air. "You may not want me when I..."

He interrupts me. "I will always want you. I've tried to think of every reason the past eighteen months not to be with you. I can't fight it anymore. You are all that I want, all that I need. There is nothing," He lifts my chin, so I must look directly at him. "and I mean *nothing* that you must work through and tell me about later that will change my wanting you." His eyes search for my understanding.

Through more sobs I attempt to speak. "You don't know that. It's big, it's huge. It's not something you will consider no big deal. You'll feel differently about me. I know you will. It's that bad."

He wipes my tears before engulfing my mouth with his. His kiss demonstrates his declaration to me. It proves his conviction as he attempts to swallow my fear, my guilt, and my doubt. He attempts to fill my heart and mind with his love for me and the knowledge that he will always want me. It's a passionate kiss, but not in a sexual way. His passion is for me and for us. My crying stops. I cling to the hope that there just might be a chance.

I squeal as Hamilton tugs the towel from my body. Our eyes lock in the vanity mirror. In his I find feral desire. He spins me, lifts me, and carries me back to his bed.

I giggle as he gently tosses me to the mattress then leans atop me.

"Hamilton, your mother will be back any minute." I attempt to be the voice of maturity in this moment.

He blatantly ignores my mention of his mother's return. Instead he removes his shirt and jeans while peppering kisses on my lips, my neck, my collarbone, and my ribcage.

At the sudden absence of his mouth, my eyes open. He's smiling while his eyes skim my face. His lips slightly part.

"You are so beautiful." His molten brown eyes sparkle. They match his dazzling smile. His dark wavy hair has grown too long—I can't keep my fingers from tangling in it. His dark stubble is more than evading the razor for a day or two. It's soft and prickly at the same time. His brown eyes, I could swim in their chocolate depths forever. And his body, oh his body, has only improved with time. Although always muscular and strong, it's now defined and powerful. He now sports dips and contours as his soft skin covers the rock-hard muscles. I rapidly blink to regain focus on Hamilton's words.

"Welcome back," he teases. "I've always known you are beautiful inside and out. They say absence makes the heart grow fonder—it's cheesy, but it's true." Hamilton places a gentle kiss upon the corner of my mouth. "It seems our distance apart caused my true feelings for you to surface."

"Or my sexual prowess on our one night together..." I attempt to tease, but he places his fingertips on my lips.

He replaces his fingers with his mouth. My brain grows quiet and I feel. I bask in every glorious sensation he awards me. I moan softly when his strong hands part my thighs and his hot tongue darts to tickle my clit. My back arches and my fingers clutch hold of his soft waves. His strong palm flattens to my abdomen in an attempt to halt my thrashing. His hot breath assails my sensitive nub when he blows for a moment before he lightly scrapes with his whiskered chin. I cry out at the overwhelming sensation. Sensing my approval, he repeats the warm wet lick, the hot breeze, then the tantalizing torture of his stubble—once, twice, and I cum.

Like a sniper's bullet I am not prepared. I scream as my every muscle tightens then spasms, my head burrows into the mattress, I grind my pelvis against him, and shatter into a sextillion pieces.

I'm lost in a sea of sensations while he nips, licks, and kisses his way over my stomach, my breasts, my neck, to my mouth. I lazily return his kiss.

I finally summon the strength to partially open my eyes. He's there, inches from me a proud smirk upon his face. I swat his shoulder begging him to stop. When he doesn't, I take our situation into my own hands, literally.

I firmly grasp him in my palm. My treacherous body outs me. I quiver. I'm trying to harness my inner-sex vixen and I quiver at the anticipation of his heavy cock about to enter me. I focus on my task. I watch his pupils dilate as I apply pressure with each stroke. I position my thumb upon the ridged nerve on the underside enjoying the groan I evoke while his eyes close. My fingertips slide the slick drop of pre-cum over his tip.

I gasp suddenly rolled over and impaled upon the cock I massaged in my hand the moment before. My fingertips bite into his pecs as I adapt to the full sensation. Hamilton's hands on my ass urge me to move.

While my hips grind, my eyes beg his to love me. I urge them to love me in spite of my secret, and to love me and our daughter. His eyes seem to be talking to mine at the same time.

Tears well in my eyes at the realization while our hearts and bodies communicate our eyes display the secrets we withhold. When wetness escapes to my cheeks, Hamilton's thumbs swipe them away as his fingers hold my jaws.

With an ab crunch his lips rise to mine. He presses his forehead to mine while whispering everything will be okay.

41

MADISON

Promptly at 3:00 p.m. the organ music announces it's time for us to walk down the aisle to witness Salem and Latham's vows. The church is toasty warm thanks to a service man agreeing to work off the clock on a Friday night to ensure the wedding would go on without a hitch.

As I walk down the aisle, my eyes find Hamilton looking sharper than James Bond in his black tux. He smiles warmly and winks before I turn to take my spot on the step leading to the altar.

The music changes, the crowd stands and Salem on her father's arm beams as she walks to Latham at the front of the church. I see a hint of tears in her eyes as Latham accepts her hand from her father. Latham looks scared to death, his face is pale, and he stands stiffly.

When I spoke to him earlier he seemed like the normal farm boy he is. He admitted to fighting his hangover all day but felt fine for the ceremony. I glance at Winston. He wins first-place for the worst hangover today. He still looks a bit green in his tux. Adrian complained about what a big baby he had been all night.

Hamilton and I walk out arm in arm. Once in the sanctuary Hamilton spins me towards him. He tells me how ravishing I look before kissing me passionately in front of all of our friends. This is not a peck on the forehead or the cheek. It's a panty melting-if I were wearing any, heartbeat skipping, melting into a puddle of wanton need, long smoldering kiss. I strain to reopen my eyes. Our group of friends stand statue still, mouths agape in shock by Hamilton's actions.

"Now, that's more like it," Adrian cheers while clapping. Walking closer to us she continues, "The two of you have skated around this for years. It was exhausting to witness. Now, sleep together and live happily ever after."

I bury my face in Hamilton's chest. My cheeks burn with embarrassment. We are in a church for goodness sake. The girl has no shame and most of the time no filter. When I finally pull away from Hamilton, I find our friends gathered tightly around us. It seems Hamilton's public profession of feelings for me is well received.

Adrian places us in a receiving line as guests begin to spill into the reception hall. Hamilton keeps his hand on the small of my back as we welcome Salem and Latham's family and friends. Salem kept her wedding small—the ceremony and reception are intimate for all in attendance.

As I enjoy dinner at the wedding party table, I realize for the first time that Salem and Latham are truly the epitome of high school sweethearts. It's the captain and quarterback of the football team falling in love with the head cheerleader. Many books and movies exist based on such a couple.

My mind then wanders to Hamilton and me. Not that we are officially a couple or anything. Yet. I hope we will be someday. We are the tumultuous storyline of the popular jock with the nerd. Hamilton as my high school friend thought his job was to pry me away from my books and laptop to attend events with him. I was his nerdy sidekick and he was my fun-loving, center-of-attention hero. Wow, our journey has yet to begin and I am already writing our story. I shake away my thoughts, drawing my attention back to the couple of the hour-Salem and Latham.

Music plays during the reception, however there is no dance floor or first dance. Salem opted for the traditional meal, cake cutting, and at the end the tossing the garter and bouquet. With the holidays mere days away, she knew families were busy and wanted to keep the ceremony and reception short. I'm grateful as it allows me to return to Columbia at a decent hour. I long to hold Liberty in my arms.

Adrian loudly announces it's time for the single ladies and guys to gather. She escorts me to the front of the women beside Savannah. "You're next," she whispers in my ear. "You better catch the damn bouquet or feel my wrath."

"Pregnancy doesn't agree with you," I tease.

I have no intention of catching Salem's flowers. My life is complicated enough without everyone claiming I am the next to be married. It's time for me to focus on my new career and my daughter. And of course, Hamilton's public display of affection will haunt my thoughts for many months to come.

Latham lifts Salem's dress, removing her garter with only his teeth amidst cheers. He shoots it like a rubber band from his fingers. It lands on Hamilton's head. The white and red garter sits as a crown upon his dark locks. He quickly grabs it and hands it to a teenage boy standing beside him. Several adults inform him he can't pass it, he's the next to marry. Hamilton's eyes dart my direction. Giggling, I can only shrug.

Adrian makes a big production of adjusting the line of all the single ladies before she passes the bouquet to Salem. Of course, Savannah and I are front and center. Salem turns her back, as the crowd counts one, two, three she then tosses it over her head to the right of us ladies. It falls at the feet of a man before Salem's single cousin hurries to claim it. Yay, she's the next to marry.

Shortly after Salem and Latham make their escape, I say my goodbyes. Hamilton walks me to my car prolonging our goodbye. He promises to visit me before he heads to Mesa in January as he pulls me closer. He kisses the top of my head while holding me in the chilly air. He begs me to stay one more night and drive home tomorrow in the daylight, but I can't bear to spend another night away from Liberty. I claim I need to help Alma as her family begins arriving.

42

HAMILTON

I stand frozen in the church parking lot watching as my heart and world drive away. I mentally kick myself for only completing half of my goal this weekend. I'm not sure I successfully demonstrated how much Madison means to me. While I left no doubt my physical attractions to her, I didn't ask her to come to Chicago, to live with me, and start our lives together.

Instead, I let her excitement for her life and new job in Columbia keep me from telling her everything.

Now, I'll spend the rest of the off-season alone and pining for Madison from too many miles away.

43

MADISON

As I begin to drive through Athens, I head West instead of South. I drive unaware of my destination. Ten minutes later I pull into my mother's drive. It's 6:30 p.m. on a Saturday, I knew she wouldn't be home. I walk through the unlocked front door. Empty bottles no longer decorate only her bedroom. The living room and kitchen are cluttered with her remnants. My heart aches at the confirmation that nothing has changed in her life. My absence doesn't cause her to reach out or visit me. For my mother the entire universe revolves around her.

Briskly I flee from my former home to the safety of my car. I set my course for Columbia and my new family. A family that needs me, supports me, and misses me when I am away. A family I depend on as they depend on me. My new family and my new life far away from my mother.

Like my drive home from Adrian and Winston's wedding, my mind attempts to process my new reality, my lovely daughter, my new job, and Hamilton's actions. I count all of my blessings before I ponder all things to do with Hamilton. His kiss made it clear to everyone that he considers me more than a friend. I must wait for his next text or phone call to see where he plans our relationship to go.

Long distance relationships suck. *Will he really move us forward? Will he treat me like a girlfriend? How will our friendship change?* I fear that he might follow through on his promise to surprise me with a visit before he heads to Arizona. I must arrange for us to meet in Athens if he mentions it again.

I know I should load Liberty in my car, drive to Athens, and immediately share my secret with Hamilton. I vowed to reveal our daughter to him prior to the start of next baseball season—I'm down to one month, now. I have two major focuses for January. I start my new job and I need to introduce Liberty to her father in the next thirty days.

Alma's home fills with family and excitement as Christmas morning arrives. Keeping her family tradition, we gather around the Christmas tree to open presents still in our pajamas. Alma dawns her Santa hat while passing out gifts. Her grandchildren make it their mission to teach Liberty to open gifts.

My daughter giggles and claps while watching others rip gift wrap to reveal the present beneath. The boys pull a corner open for Libby to grab. She simply looks to them to finish the task for her. Trenton and Taylor's children decide it's easier for them to open the gifts and allow Liberty to cheer them on. They assist in removing new toys from their boxes, so she may play with them.

I save her gifts from her daddy in my room to open later in front of the webcam.

Waking I groan. I lie completely still willing myself back to sleep, back to my dream. Of course, this never works. Now staring at the ceiling, I smile remembering the warmth of Hamilton's arms when he held me next to our Christmas tree. It's the kind of dream I never want to end.

Hamilton and I played Santa after our four-year-old daughter fell asleep. While he assembled her little bicycle with tassels, a bell, a basket, and training wheels; I filled her stocking and placed other gifts under the tree. We laughed and teased while reading and rereading the instructions to assemble the bike. He vowed to pay extra for assembly from now on.

With Santa gifts all ready, we each nibbled a cookie from Santa's plate and chased it down with milk. Hamilton pointed out we were positioned below the mistletoe. That's where I woke up. I was snuggled in his arms as we kissed under the mistletoe.

As upset as I am the dream ended, I'm grateful it wasn't a nightmare as many of my dreams seem to be lately.

44

MADISON

As I assist Alma dusting the house during Liberty's nap time, my cell phone rings with an unknown number.

"Hello, this is Madison," I answer. It's the principal from the middle school I'll be starting as a long-term substitute teacher in three days. I take a seat allowing myself to give him my full attention. As he explains they won't be needing me to cover this placement, a hot heavy weight lands in the pit of my stomach. I listen while he explains the male teacher I was to cover for will no longer need to take five weeks off for paternity leave. His wife gave birth three weeks early.

Tears sting my eyes as I assure him I understand that babies rarely arrive as scheduled and I hope he will keep me in mind for any upcoming subs he might need.

As I return my phone to my back pocket, I mourn the loss of the steady income I counted on for the next five weeks.

I return the duster to the pantry before filling Alma in on my disappointing phone conversation. I excuse myself to my bedroom as I need to register for substitute positions at the area school districts.

For the next three hours, I jump from website to website inputting my information and uploading my documentation. I download the two mobile apps most districts use so I am ready to receive alerts as openings occur.

Now I wait. Several schools restart classes from winter break tomorrow, so I need to be ready to quickly accept any openings that might alert me tonight or prior to seven in the morning.

I shoot a text to Hamilton as I head downstairs to join Alma and my girl.

Me: sub job cancelled
Me: (sad emoji)

I say goodnight to Alma as I carry Liberty up to bed. Liberty and I rock for fifteen minutes before I lay my sleeping girl in her crib.

I slip into my pajamas before climbing into bed with a notebook and my laptop in hand. I start a random movie on Netflix, take my pen in hand, and start writing. Instead of continuing my story, I journal tonight. I fill pages with my disappointment. I complain now that instead of one school, one subject, and one group of students for five weeks, I will be at different schools, with different ages or subjects, and new students every day.

I'll no longer know if I work tomorrow or in three days—at times I'll get an alert or phone call then need to be at the classroom within an hour.

I looked forward to this long-term placement to make a great impression day after day. Now it might be harder to meet influential administrators at each building while I'm only there a day then not seen again for a while.

I really thought this was my lucky break. I wanted this chance to fit in as a part of a team, it's not easy to do that one day here and one day there.

I pout and wallow in my disappointment for several hours before finally falling asleep with Netflix still streaming on my laptop.

45

MADISON

Day after day and night after night, I attempt to accept sub positions when alerted to an opening. It seems many other subs are much faster than me at accepting a sub job. Over and over, I'm notified the position has already been filled when I reply to an alert.

After two weeks, I finally successfully accept a sub position. Tomorrow I am a kindergarten teacher in an elementary school on the far side of Columbia. Tonight, instead of fretting about my finances and ability to find a teaching position for fall, the worry of the unknown keeps me awake. The thought of successfully entertaining twenty-one five-year-olds for seven hours scares me. I should be excited to work and earn money, but I dread it.

Getting up early to drive thirty-five minutes across town exhausts me just thinking about it. I want easy. I want comfortable. I want to stay home with Liberty and not be seen in public, but I need to work.

46

MADISON

Try as I might, I cannot shake last night's nightmare. The images replay all day. It's one of my biggest fears. I often worry as I keep putting off telling Hamilton that I might pass the point of no return. In the dream, Liberty started kindergarten and I still hadn't introduced the two of them. I kept finding an excuse not to reveal his daughter to him. Today I've imagined my life as a single mother of a middle school and high school daughter. I draw on my own years without a father.

I don't want Liberty to watch her friends with their fathers and yearn for hers. I don't want her to go without. I don't want him to miss the little things in her life. As it is now, he'll miss the first two years. He's missed a lot already—I need to ensure he doesn't miss another year of firsts.

It's here. Today's the day all single, widowed, and divorced women dread most. We can't hide from our calendars—it's February 14th. Alma asked me not to accept a sub position for today. She has secret plans for the two of us while Liberty attends Mother's Day Out Preschool at our church.

As I walk down to breakfast, I silently hope our five hours aren't as painful as the commercials leading up to this holiday are to watch. As difficult as it is on us unattached females, it must be equally stressful for attached men. The ads guilt them into needing to buy their special someone jewelry, expensive perfume, extravagant floral arrangements, and luxury cars. While each ad reminds me like a slap in the face that I'm single, the ads must remind men they need to take out a loan to prove they love their women.

Alma playfully reminds Liberty our plans are a secret as I enter the kitchen. I approach the highchair and place good morning kisses on my daughter's cheek. I play along by asking Liberty what secret plans Alma confessed to her.

I realize Alma only wants me to enjoy the day, but we are different. She's known true love, she experienced decades of love with her husband. While I love, I have to experience a year with someone I love, let alone decades. While Alma reflects upon memories, I long to have a relationship I've read about or one the commercials portray.

I try multiple times to ask Alma about her plans. She's closed up tight like Fort Knox.

We walk Liberty into her classroom together. Alma says her goodbye in the hall before I walk Liberty in to her teacher. Once entering the classroom, it's as if I no longer exist. Liberty loves playtime with her friends. I worry she spends too much time in the company of adults. Seeing her interact with children her age does my heart good. She's outgoing, friendly, and kind to everyone.

As we return to the van, I ask Alma one more time about our plans. She zips her lips with pinched fingers and pretends to toss the key over her shoulder while wearing a sly grin.

With every turn through the streets of Columbia I quickly edit the list of possible activities she might be driving me towards. I breathe a sigh of relief when we park at a movie theater. If we spend two hours of our five free hours today at a movie, perhaps Alma's Valentine's Day plans won't be bad.

Alma purchases two tickets to a comedy containing one of her favorite hunky young male actors. She turns right instead of heading straight to our theater. I assume we need popcorn and colas, but instead of the counter she leans on the bar.

"Two long Island iced teas, please."

The bartender nods. He asks which movie we plan to see. He claims he's heard many great things about our comedy. As we prepare to leave, Alma shares our theater number and assigned seats, stating we'll need two refills each spread throughout our movie.

I can only shake my head when he agrees. Patrons usually exit a movie to procure a refill. This is so Alma—she's loved by everyone. It's hard not to entertain her. The bar staff will deliver our two sets of refills just as I will drink the three Long Island iced teas she ordered for me. It seems Alma plans to get me tipsy today.

We laugh so hard during our movie that I snort twice. I'm glad on a weekday the theater is nearly empty. Alma loudly cheers during her hunks nearly naked scenes further drawing attention to us. We spend most of the movie fanning our over-heated faces.

As we giggle and lean into each other in the lobby, a college-age male approaches. I recall seeing him at church functions. It seems Alma arranged him as our Uber driver until 3 p.m. today. It's now I realize neither of us should drive with the drinks we enjoyed. The alcohol didn't affect Alma enough to let me know where we head next.

Our driver easily escorts us to a strip-mall a couple of miles from the theater. Alma instructs him to pick us up at 2:45 p.m. I guess we will shop for the two and a half hours until we pick up Liberty at three.

As she planned our adventure today, I allow Alma to lead as we glance in each storefront. We pass two clothing boutiques and a hobby shop before Alma holds a door open for me to enter the Ink, Inc. Tattoo Shoppe.

I recall Alma confessing a few weeks ago that she's often thought of getting a tattoo. I thought about it several times since then, but never mentioned it to her. She must be ready to do it today.

When Alma states she's finally getting her tattoo and I can watch, I announce I want one, too. I love the large knowing smile that graces her face. "I'd hoped you would say that. Your first tattoo is on me."

"Hello, ladies," a thirty-something heavily tattooed blonde greets approaching the counter. "I'm Wyatt. Which one of you wants a tat today?"

I scan my eyes from his sandy blonde man bun to just below his waist where the counter obstructs my view. He's muscular but not bulky—he reminds me of Latham in his build. I've always found tattoos sexy when they don't take up every inch of skin. It's clear Wyatt likes tattoos to express himself but hasn't gone overboard. Matching sleeves from mid-forearm decorate up to disappear under his short-sleeved black skin-tight t-shirt. They contain no color, just black and shades of gray creating the Filipino Tribal designs. His only other visible art catches my eye. Low on his neck a half-dollar size, black and red Star Wars design sparks my interest. I point toward his neck while asking if I might examine it closer.

Wyatt places his forearms on the glass countertop and leans toward me. Half the circle is part of the Rebels' Logo and half is the Empire's Logo. Three heavy-poured drinks disabled my filters. I trace my fingertips on the design while biting my lip.

"It's a Star Wars design," Wyatt states a sexy smirk on his lips.

It's clear he doesn't think I know. "Which way do you lean?" I whisper. Yes, I whisper. *What's up with that?*

Alma clears her throat attempting to pull me from my actions.

"Light Side vs Dark Side, Jedi vs. Sith, Rebels vs. Empire," I ask out loud my voice stronger now. "I tend to lean to the Light Side while the Dark Side attempts to creep in at night." My hand covers my mouth as I realize how my words might be interpreted. Through my fingers I explain, "I struggle with depression. Its darkness threatens 24/7, but I'm weakest to its influence at night."

Wyatt's blue eyes darken with my words. It's easy to see he appreciates my extensive knowledge of Star Wars and its resemblance to my life. I believe he knows I compare my struggles with that of Anakin Skywalker's before becoming Darth Vader.

Alma interrupts. "Both of us want tattoos today."

Wyatt stands once again speaking to Alma. "Feel free to browse the walls and these portfolios for ideas. Either of you already have art?" His dark blue eyes scan my body for hints of previous work.

"I already know what I want for my first tattoo." Alma looks to me. "My friend might need help to decide on her first."

I shake my head. "I have an idea. Do you do original designs?"

"Noel, we've got virgin skin for you." Wyatt hollers toward the back.

A gorgeous young woman peeks over the cubicles smiling, then cheers before joining us in the front.

Wyatt and Alma chat for a bit, then he secures a page from a binder on the front counter to show her. She nods and the two disappear to his station while Noel pulls a sketchpad and pencils from under the counter. "What are you envisioning?" I watch her take notes at the bottom of the page as I explain.

"I'd like a left-handed pitcher gripping a baseball ready to throw a four-seam fastball." I admire her hazel eyes with artistically applied eye shadow to further make the green pop. Her left eyebrow contains two silver hoops with tiny blue and green striped beads. Looking down I marvel at the speed in which she sketches a baseball. I startle when she hollers for Wyatt's help.

"Show me how to hold a baseball for a..." Noel's eyes glance at the bottom of her page. "A four-seam fastball." Her voice rises with her last word. She's clearly not an avid baseball fan. It's not fair to judge her, as most women aren't as versed in pitches as I am.

"If you have a ball I can show you," I offer. "I'm not sure how to explain it without actually seeing it."

Wyatt produces a weathered baseball from a tub under the counter. I chuckle as it seems weird to find a baseball in a tattoo shop. Wyatt explains it was found in the parking lot and they decided to keep it for situations just like this. He expertly positions his hand to demonstrate, while looking to me for confirmation. When I nod, he admits he pitched a bit in high school. Knowing the difference between a two- and four-seam fastball leads me to believe he pitched more than a bit. His interest peaked, Wyatt stays to see the design I chose.

Noel returns to sketching, "Glad Wyatt's a lefty. It makes visualization easier."

"I'd like the fingers in black, red stitching on the baseball, and a royal blue #1 Fan on the face of the ball."

"Nice," Wyatt praises before returning to Alma.

Noel's dimples decorate her cheeks and her eyes twinkle before her hand returns to sketching. "I love creating permanent artwork that means something to my client. Can you tell me why you chose this design? The more I know the better I can help the image come to life."

I tell her about my best friend, our high school friendship, and his teams. I'm careful not to divulge his name or which MLB team he plays for. I only share enough to help her create my image. I'm aware assuming he's from Missouri, it wouldn't be hard to find a left-handed pitcher from Missouri currently in the Majors, but Noel doesn't seem the type to put that much work into finding out anything about a sport.

I marvel at the effortless ease in which she sketches my design. "Does he still know you're his number one fan?" I nod. "Cool." She turns her sketch to face me. "Maybe one day you'll share your tattoo with him and he'll fall in love with you as much as you are in love with him."

Noel is *very* intuitive. *Or am I that easy to read?*

As she ushers me to her cubicle she asks where I plan to place the design. I point to my left front jeans pocket. I explain I want to be the only one to see it. She shows me where to lay and instructs me to lower my jeans and underwear to reveal the entire area. I'm glad my body faces the wall, so I won't be on display to anyone walking by.

I listen as she tugs on her black gloves and explains the safety precautions while cleaning my skin. She asks me to place my fingertips where I want the top and bottom of the baseball. She places a tiny ink pen dot at these two locations.

With equipment in hand she asks me if I'm ready. When I

nervously nod she mumbles 'virgin' while shaking her head and placing the needle to my skin. I grind my teeth while holding my breath as needles inflict sharp, scratching pain upon my skin. I let out my breath and relax my jaw as I now know what to expect in terms of pain level.

I can handle this intense scratchy feeling. I had imagined extreme pain like labor pains—this is much easier. I smile realizing Hamilton will be a permanent part of me. My tattoo will remind me of his high school, minor, and major league career while also reminding me the reason I chose to keep our daughter a secret for a few years.

To anyone lucky enough to catch a glimpse of my tattoo in the future, they will only believe I am a big baseball fan. Those who know me well will know that the left hand belongs to Hamilton and could be no one else.

Noel remains quiet as she works. I enjoy the rush of adrenaline the constant pain releases. I now understand how some claim tattoos may become addictive. I feel alive.

Hamilton's FaceTime call pulls my attention from my writing. My laptop clock tells me it's 9:30 p.m. I position my pillows against my headboard as I answer.

Hamilton shares about his first day of practice with the other pitchers and catchers as they reported today. He then wishes me a Happy Valentine's Day. We discuss as we had last year how much it sucks to be alone tonight. He asks how my day was.

"Alma planned a movie and surprise shopping trip for me today."

"What movie?" Hamilton repositions himself to lie on his side facing his tablet camera.

Instead of answering I blurt, "We got tattoos!"

I watch Hamilton thin his lips between his teeth and furrow his brow. I continue, "Instead of shopping, Alma wanted to finally get her tattoo, so I got one, too."

When he asks what I got and for me to show it to him, I explain it's in a private location and only meant for me to see. He begs a couple of more times before realizing I won't share details tonight.

I shouldn't have blurted it out. I knew I wouldn't want to share the details. I wanted him to know how daring I was today, but now I realize I will field questions about my tattoo until I cave and show him. I'm grateful Hamilton states he needs to turn in and ends our call.

47

HAMILTON

Madison got a tattoo.

Now said tattoo haunts me as I try to fall asleep. My sex-starved mind imagines its location. If it had been on her arm, neck, wrist, or legs she would have shown me, or I might have seen a bandage.

Maybe it's on her ribcage and curves under her breast. I groan remembering how fine her breasts are. I bet it's some saying or quote that means something to her. I imagine her lying in my bed. As I kiss her, I unfasten and remove her lacy black bra. I trail my lips down her collarbone and around her globes. A I plan to attend to her nipple, I freeze when I glimpse the script. I trace my fingertip over each letter. Madison wriggles as my featherlight touch tickles.

My mind leaps to another option. Perhaps her tattoo is instead a red heart with words upon a scroll woven through it. As I remove her red satin panties, I spy the tattoo low, and I mean low, on her abdomen near her right hip. Her tiny panties kept the treasure hidden. First, I trace the design with my fingers then my tongue while gazing up at her face through my lashes. Her head presses back into the mattress and her back arches in pleasure.

Why didn't I stay on the phone until she gave in and showed me her new tattoo? At least then I wouldn't imagine it on every part of her soft skin. The subject of the tattoo isn't as distracting as its location is for me. My mind constantly fantasizes about Madison before the mention of a tattoo. Now my previous knowledge of her body combined with a mysterious tattoo overload my senses.

I'm never going to fall asleep this way. I contemplate calling her back to find the answers to my tattoo questions. Even if we speak, I'd still be in my current state afterwards.

I decide I must take the matter into my own hands. Literally. I opt for a shower instead of my bed. When steam fills the room, I step inside my glass shower. The hot water immediately caresses every inch of my skin. I imagine the droplets are Madison's fingertips exploring every part of me.

I squirt a drop of body wash into my palm. Slowly I glide one hand over my erect cock and groan at the sensation. My eyelids close and my head tips back as my second hand joins my first. I tighten my fist working up and down as my right-hand swirls lightly over my crown.

After an hour and a half of fantasizing in my bed and a few pumps of my fist, I'm near the edge. I lower my gaze to my left hand pumping my cock and slam my right hand on the glass wall to balance myself. I lean into my palm, rising to my toes for my final thrust as I growl Madison's name. Cumming I shudder once, twice, then a final stream of semen spurts onto the glass in front of me.

With both hands pressed on the wall, I attempt to remain standing in the wake of my release. The shower stream pummels my back and water covers every part of me. I allow myself five minutes under the relaxing spray before lathering my entire body and rinsing off.

My mind remains on Madison when I crawl back into bed, but I'm at ease. Sleep sweeps me off to dreams of moving Madison to Chicago, getting engaged, and finally starting our lives together.

48

MADISON

I shoot up from my bed. Taking in my surroundings I find I'm in my room covered from head to toe in sweat. It felt real. It was my reoccurring dream of telling Hamilton about Liberty. In tonight's episode even after meeting her, he demands a paternity test. He accuses me of becoming pregnant on purpose to get his money.

My tight chest aches with the accusation and lack of trust. I'm hurt that my closest friend might ever believe I could do such things. I know keeping my secret will cause others not to trust me in the future, but I hope that everyone will believe me when I admit Liberty is Hamilton's daughter.

49

MADISON

It's now March and I cannot believe Liberty will be one this month. The first twelve months of her life flew by. As did the off-season in which I didn't keep my promise to introduce Hamilton to his daughter. His agent kept him busy claiming remaining in the public eye keeps him in demand. Hamilton complains his agent's favorite words are 'strike while the iron is hot.' Hamilton is now back in Arizona. I know. I know. I conveniently keep putting it off.

"Have a seat," Alma greets as I enter the kitchen to prepare dinner.

"Would you like me to start dinner first?" I try to interpret Alma's stern demeanor. Is she ill or in pain? I worry about her health more with each passing day. I fear what will come of Liberty and me should something happen to her.

"We'll order pizza after we talk."

Oh no. This sounds ominous. I take a seat across from her, place my arms on the table, and tip my head for her to begin.

"When do you plan to tell Hamilton?" Alma's eyes peer into mine. Alma knows Hamilton is already in Mesa, Arizona. He returned early just as he did last year.

"I guess I'll have to wait until next October to introduce Hamilton to her." I rest my chin in my hands with elbows on the table. "I'll tell him before Liberty turns two. I can't let it go any farther than that." I inhale deeply. "Will you make sure I tell him before next Christmas?" Perhaps I can count on her to force me to keep my word. I know she will hold me accountable.

Alma rises from her chair. She remains silent until she returns with two water bottles. She slides one over to me. "That's a long time away, are you sure you don't want to travel to Mesa now?"

If I fly to Arizona this week or next, I'd interrupt Hamilton's pre-season routines. I'd need to take Liberty with me, so Alma would need to tag along. Regardless of Hamilton's reaction to my revealing he has a daughter, this close to his season would interfere with his performance for the months that follow.

"I can't upset his world right as his pre-season starts. This is life-altering news. He needs time to process it. I have to do it during next off-season." My eyes beg Alma to validate my reasoning.

"Then next October, November, or December it will be." I breathe easier knowing she agrees. "Let's formally invite Hamilton and his family here for Christmas. We have plenty of room for three more and once he meets his daughter he will want to be near her for the holiday."

I like the idea of my two families sharing the holiday.

"When I call Memphis," Alma continues. "I'll mention you feel torn between the two families at the holidays. Perhaps that will encourage them to accept the invitation."

We discuss reaching out to Memphis in July, securing a hotel nearby for Alma's children, and now that we have a firm date in mind we can plan in greater detail as fall approaches. Alma writes on her July calendar to call Memphis about Christmas. I create an event in my iCal. I also create the event in my countdown app for December Twenty-Fourth. This will keep a count of the total days I have until I need to meet with Hamilton. I hope I find an opportunity prior to Christmas to tell Hamilton, but if not at least with Alma's help Liberty will meet the rest of her family by Christmas.

I order pizza delivery while Alma runs Liberty's bath.

––––––––––––––

While enjoying our pizza, my phone vibrates alerting an incoming call from Adrian. It's after 7:00 p.m. I send it to voicemail hoping she'll text instead. With texting I'm able to reply when it's convenient for me and I have more time to think of my responses. Texting allows me to enjoy more time with Liberty.

At the next commercial break, I excuse myself as tears begin to sting the back of my eyes. I've cried too much lately. Liberty's new achievements cause me to cry. Missing Hamilton and my friends bring tears. Just now, a cell phone commercial brought the tears I struggle to control. I pour myself another glass of wine before blotting my eyes and wiping my cheeks. I take a couple deep, calming breaths before returning to the front room.

I'm greeted by Alma's concerned eyes. I blame these tears on hormones. She raises her brow not buying my excuse.

I sip my wine as Liberty enjoys her final minutes of playtime before bath and bed time.

––––––––––––––

Liberty's birthday is this weekend. Glancing at my cell phone I peruse my list. I've planned a simple First Birthday party for the three of us. I still need to wrap her gifts and pick up the cake otherwise, I am prepared.

Liberty's voice travels through the baby monitor alerting us she's awake from her afternoon nap. I tuck my cell phone in my pocket as I ascend the stairs. On the third step, my phone rings. I pause to answer.

"Adrian is in labor," Salem's excitement is clear. "Her water broke at ten this morning and labor is progressing quickly now. They cleared the room of everyone except Winston and Adrian's mother." We chat for a bit and Salem promises to call as soon as she has news.

I scoop Liberty from her crib into my arms. She places her hands on each side of my face and plants a wet baby kiss near my mouth.

"Adrian is having her baby today," I inform my daughter. "Her birthday will be two days before your birthday. Isn't that exciting?" Liberty claps her hands as if she knows what I say.

I opt to spend my entire evening with Alma, Libby, and McGee. I check my phone often throughout the evening. As more time passes I worry about complications and shoot a text to Salem.

Me: any news?
Salem: wheeled her for C-Section over 30 min ago
Salem: promise to text soon

I tuck Libby in bed by eight and immediately pour two glasses of wine. After two full glasses of wine, I decide to retire for the night at 9:30 p.m.

At ten, Salem texts that Adrian and baby girl are tucked safely in their room. Both mom and baby are happy and healthy. My friend doesn't know it yet, but her daughter's birthday is two days before my daughter's. My thoughts drift to the years ahead when my secret is revealed. I imagine joint birthday parties as our girls grow up one year apart. Bethany is now five months pregnant with a baby due in July. Her son or daughter will only be four months younger than Adrian's daughter. Recently Salem revealed they are trying to conceive. Last year's theme was weddings, this year's theme is babies. With all but Savannah and I married, the rest of our gang moved on to starting families.

50

MADISON

As I arrive home from my day as a middle school physical education teacher on Friday, a rental car is parked in front of Alma's house. We weren't expecting company, at least not that I knew of. As I walk up the porch steps, Cameron opens the front door and Liberty toddles out to greet me.

"Momma," Libby cheers as she wraps her arms around my leg.

I lift her in my arms while walking toward Cameron. "What are you doing here?" I suddenly worry we had an editor's meeting I might have forgotten.

Cameron steals Libby from me. "I couldn't miss my niece's first birthday."

I shake my head. *When will I ever learn to expect these family surprises?* After dinner a knock at the door has Alma hopping from her chair. Trenton, Taylor, and their families spill into the house. Alma's grandchildren scramble to Libby playing on the floor.

"Am I the only one surprised here?" I ask Alma.

She explains they planned during the Christmas visit to surprise Libby and me for her first birthday. Tears well in my eyes as I realize the only thing missing will be Hamilton.

Mid-morning Saturday, Bethany's video call rings my phone. She immediately asks to see the birthday girl. I attempt to chat with Bethany as I follow behind Liberty with camera in hand as she plays with the other kids.

Bethany shares that Troy's over-protectiveness has reached a new level. At five months pregnant he now worries about pre-term labor, Bethany falling due to the size of her belly, and hurting the baby while having sex. He doesn't want her driving and insists to drive her anywhere she needs to go. He's scheduled drop-in visits each afternoon by his and her parents, to make sure she's okay.

I try to help her understand he's an excited first-time dad. He's trying to protect his family and although it's a bit over the top, he does it because he loves her. I encourage her to express her frustration and for the two of them to plan ways to let him know all is okay throughout the day, while allowing her to continue her daily activities. I mention she could text him often, sometimes even just an emoji to let him know all is well.

With pregnancy hormones always in control, Bethany mentions sending him an eggplant emoji and several others to suggest he hurry home and carry her off to bed. I reprimand her for talking about sex on Liberty's birthday phone call.

At the mention of my daughter, Bethany complains she had to share her attention today with Alma's family. I corral my daughter in her nursery allowing Bethany a few minutes of Libby's attention and to wish her a happy birthday before we end our call.

To ensure no other random phone calls interrupt Liberty's party, I text Hamilton setting up a call with him after nine tonight when I am alone in my bedroom. This allows me to enjoy Liberty's birthday without the worry he'll call and wonder what all the family is doing here this weekend.

Weeks later, the bathroom mirror cruelly reflects my image back at me. With little sleep last night, I opted to skip washing my hair to lie in bed fifteen extra minutes. Dark circles like bruises under my eyes broadcast my weeks of insomnia. I make it through each day with caffeine constantly in hand.

By 8:00 p.m. I'm ready for bed. Once there, sleep refuses to arrive. Some nights I lie with my eyes closed in the dark for hours in hopes of sleep. As that fails, most nights I write. I figure I won't be able to sleep for hours, I might as well be productive.

My new curse is a mind constantly creating two or more stories at once. The more I write the more story ideas spark to life. For every story I complete two more take its place. I have one notebook containing lists of future story ideas—it's growing fuller by the day.

I'm proud of my notebooks full of stories. Writing unclogs my head, works through my issues, and helps lighten my dark moods.

―――――――

A FaceTime call vibrates my phone. It's Hamilton. It's been almost a month since our last call. I prop my phone on the pillow beside mine as I answer.

His tired brown eyes and a lazy smile greet me. "Hey."

"You look sleepy," I force a smile hoping it hides my own exhaustion.

"I needed to see you before I fall asleep tonight," he confesses. "I didn't wake you, did I?"

"Nope. I haven't been sleeping much." I yawn, "How was today's practice?"

Our conversation flows from our plans for the week, to what little we've heard from Athens, to how much he misses me. Hamilton apologizes for how busy he's been and states. I'm always on his mind. We close each call by sharing an 'I love you'.

I'm not sure the true meaning of his three little words. Once I believed we were becoming more than friends, as time passes and the distance between us grows ominous although we continue to say, 'I love you', I worry the meaning has dissipated.

Opening my phone, I confirm I'm not imagining it. Hamilton's texts transition to fewer texts and are farther apart. Last week he texted two times and this week we've only chatted once.

I scroll further back. As I read our past conversations, I witness our interactions from Adrian's wedding all sweet and lengthy morph to quick chats of work and school then only a couple of words. Our long texts chats and calls now more often than not read 'I love you' or 'I miss you'. As time passes, we withdraw but continue to let each other know we still think of each other.

It's easier this way. Although I miss him so much it hurts, for now it's easier to hide Liberty with fewer calls where he might hear my secret in my voice or written on my face. I don't like hiding her—I regret keeping my secret. I'm taking the chicken way out to make it easier on me.

51

MADISON

I pull my cell phone close as I attempt to open my eyes. The April sunshine is bright through the blinds I forgot to close last night. *It's 9:15!* I hop from my bed and hurry to Liberty's crib. It's empty—Alma must already have her downstairs allowing me to sleep late. A gift every mom loves.

I find Liberty in her high chair munching on her cereal and Alma reading the newspaper with coffee in hand nearby. I pour a mug of coffee while I wait for my toast to brown. Liberty cheers when the toaster pops up.

I secure my hair in my usual ponytail. It allows me to go an extra day or two between washing it. I spend my extra minutes each morning lying in bed or cuddling Liberty.

Today I wear a long-sleeved T-shirt under my blouse. Along with added warmth, it fit better over its thickness. I need to ask Alma to help me shop for more this weekend. Just the thought of shopping exhausts me. I sigh as it's a necessary evil.

Today I cover high school woods class. I'm nervous thinking of all the ways teenagers can injure themselves with tools and saws while under my care. If I were more secure financially I would only select positions I felt comfortable in. Subbing three or four times a week will not fill my checking account and let me be picky, so today I will be a high school woods teacher.

———————

I check Hamilton's texts from this morning. As I know his baseball schedule, Hamilton now texts me only the reasons he's too busy to call. 'Photo shoot tomorrow', 'hospital visits today', 'dinner and contracts tomorrow with' this company or that one—his texts are meant to let me know how busy he is when he can't call. Instead they further prove me right in allowing him more time to acclimate before I reveal his daughter to him.

———————

At dinner I relive our outdoor day. I wish I could plan more days like this with Liberty and Alma. I'm lost in memories and thoughts.

"Madison," Alma interrupts our silent dinner. "Are you feeling okay?" She tilts her head and furrows her brow.

I inform her I'm fine and just tired. My appetite grows smaller when I'm tired, and I've been tired a lot lately.

"You rarely eat. Your clothes are starting to hang on you. And you weren't heavy to begin with."

I hear her real meaning. She's worried. My constant lack of energy and appetite worry her. She's reaching out in hopes of pulling me out of my ongoing funk. I don't mean to worry her. I need to make an effort to ease her worries.

———————

I cringe when Hamilton's FaceTime call rings late Sunday evening. The Cubs were home this afternoon—I should have realized there was a small chance he'd call tonight. I glance around my bed covered with notebooks scattered around me before I accept the call on my Mac with a smile upon my face.

"Wow," his warm masculine voice hugs me from afar. "You're writing I see."

"Let's chat for a few minutes then I'll let you get back to work so you don't forget what you are writing." Hamilton licks his lips before beginning. "How are you?"

Wow. Please tell me he didn't call for idle chit-chat. I don't have the patience for this.

"I'm good, just busy."

"Madison," Hamilton's tone pierces my outer armor. "It's me. I may be busy and too many miles away, but I see you. I see more than you want me to." He clears his throat and runs his fingers through his hair. "I know *it's* back and it is time you start treatment again."

My eyes sting as tears threaten. I've tried to text more than call as my appearance hints I am struggling. Hamilton and Memphis have been down this road with me a few times in the six years they've shared their home with me.

"I know you don't need me to point out how I know. So, let's move on to discussing what's going on and how we plan to work through it."

My hackles rise, and I prepare to tell him it's none of his business. How dare he try to help me from his perfect life in the spotlight high in his condo overlooking Chicago. I want to fight, I want to hang up, I want to be alone with Alma and Liberty. But I'm too tired to fight against him. I'm tired of being tired.

I wipe my tears before I nod. It's all Hamilton needs to know I'm in need of his help yet again. He offers to make appointments with my physician and counselor for me. He knows Memphis helped with this in the past.

"I saw a counselor down here last winter. I'll go online and schedule an appointment." As much as I want to curl into a ball and hide in my bed 24/7, I know from past experiences talking helps, and I need to get better for Liberty. She deserves me at my best.

"Don't!" Hamilton's adamancy startles me. "Don't go there. It's not the same and you know it."

Of course, he knew I'd compare myself to my mother. Her depression and her alcoholism took her from me after Dad's death.

"You are stronger than her," Hamilton promises. "you seek help when you need it. You do what it takes to get better." His eyes attempt to slip through my armor—they implore me to believe. "Do you want me to call Doc in Athens to get a referral? He attended Mizzou—I'm sure he knows someone close by you can see. I know you hat the side-effects, but the meds have worked in the past for you."

"I'll call Doc in the morning." Hamilton tilts his head while squinting. "I promise I will call." I put as much feeling into my words as I can. He contemplates my sincerity. I realize he is remembering me making promises in the past I didn't keep. "I'll send you a pic of my script."

Hamilton apologizes. He explains he trusts me but knows the illness might prevent me from following through. Someday I hope to be deserving of his trust. Until I share Liberty with him and begin to see my way out of the current darkness, I am not worthy of his trust.

Hamilton vows to check-in more often. He urges me to email or text anytime about anything. Although he may not be able to reply right away he promises he will read them. He asks my permission to talk to his mother about tonight's conversation. When I agree, we say goodbye and I return to writing my current story.

52

HAMILTON

S tan approaches my area in the locker room minutes before we take the field. "We still on for our post-game celebration?" he keeps his voice low, not wanting teammates to invite themselves to join us.

I nod while my eyes scan our surroundings. No one seems to care about our conversation. "The Mrs. Okay with you not coming straight home from the game?" The last thing I want is for her to kick him out again. I rather like having my condo to myself.

"She knows *how* we are celebrating and agrees I shouldn't allow you to celebrate alone." Stan pats me twice on my shoulder. "Let's go start the season of in the win-column."

I follow Stan and our teammates from the locker room onto the field. Crowds at Wrigley Field are always loud, but this Opening Day crowd is electric. Their excitement carries over from our successful season last year. We were one win away from the World Series. It's contagious. My muscles spark to life as I am introduced. I wave to my fans before assuming my position for the National Anthem.

I sing every word as I remember myself on the ball field in Athens as our announcer played a recording of the high school choir singing these same words. I love the game of baseball as much today as I did years ago.

"Here we are," Stan parks his Land Rover. "You know when you mentioned wanting to get a tattoo on opening day, I thought it was pretty lame." Stan pulls his eyes from the tattoo parlor and turns to face me in his driver's seat. "I mean the guys head to bars and night-clubs. But the more I thought about all the trouble they get into, I realized this is a much safer celebration."

"The less you hang with those guys the less trouble you get in at home," I tease remembering Stan's one-night stand last October and his wife's reaction that led to him inhabiting my sofa for several weeks.

"We gonna stay in the car like a chicken shit or are we gonna man up and ink your skin?"

I punch Stan's shoulder and exit his vehicle. I position myself with my back toward the parlor. quickly take a picture, type 'cele-brating our win', post it to Snap Chat as my story as well as, send the snap directly to Madison.

'Want me to play the role of your Instagram boyfriend to take several pictures throughout your celebration?" Stan teases. "First, we'll pose you with your hands in the shape of a heart. Then..."

"Finish that statement and I'll send a pic of you standing near a random woman to your wife."

"Not cool, man."

"Neither was your Instagram boyfriend comment." Stan pats me on the back and we enter.

53

MADISON

Alma and I share our plans for the day. It's supposed to be a warm late-April day, so I propose a long walk to the park. Alma likes my plan. When breakfast is over, I carry Libby up to change from her pajamas. We giggle and play as she attempts to run around in only her diaper. Eventually I win and wrestle her into her first outfit of the day.

Liberty and I are still laughing as we approach the top of the stairs at the same time Alma opens the front door. We made so much noise I didn't hear the doorbell. I stand frozen holding Liberty in my arms as Adrian stares at me while holding her baby carrier. My heart pounds loudly in my chest as my palms begin to sweat. Her eyes are locked on mine, there is no way she doesn't see us.

This is karma for not divulging my secret by now. I knew this day would come, I just wanted to control the narrative. I mentally berate myself for not telling Hamilton already. I gather myself as I descend the stairs. Liberty waves at our guests. Alma recognizes Adrian from our many video calls and stands frozen in the doorway. I'm sure she's as shocked as I am.

I hug Adrian awkwardly with Libby on my hip and over her baby carrier. "What are you doing all the way down here?" My voice squeaks showing my surprise. "Alma, please help Adrian come inside."

Alma snaps back to the present inviting Adrian to come in while assisting her with the diaper bag. I keep Libby on my lap to prevent her investigating the new baby.

"I missed my best friend. I spend too much time at home alone, so I decided to drive down and surprise you." She tilts her head while squinting at Libby. "But you win. Your surprise beats my surprise visit." Adrian pulls her daughter, Isabella, from her carrier.

Here we go—I can avoid this no longer. I allow my squirming daughter down and she toddles close to Adrian to get a better look. Liberty places her palms on Adrian's knees while she peeks at the sleeping infant. Alma excuses herself to the kitchen for drinks.

"She looks just like Hamilton," Adrian blurts before I may explain. "Funny though, my friend denied on more than one occasion having 'taken a nap' with him." I want to smile at her signaling air quotes with her free hand while talking in code.

"I didn't lie. I promise. If you look closely you will see there is no way that I 'took a nap' with anyone in the off season. It happened in early June before he went to Des Moines. I've wanted to tell all of you, but I have to wait until I tell him."

"Momma," Liberty's voice draws my attention. She points at the tiny baby in Adrian's arms. She looks back to me and nods her head. This is her way of asking permission.

Adrian sensing Libby's desire to see the baby suggests, "Let's give the baby to your mommy and I will help you get closer." Scooting next to me on the sofa Adrian extends her six-week-old daughter to me. "Bella, this is Madison," Adrian's voice morphs into the tone of a mother.

I cuddle her tiny, bald baby. "Hi, Bella." My free hand straightens her tiny pink headband. No doubt Adrian places it on her head so others know she is a girl. "She's so tiny."

"I'm sure this one was once that tiny," Adrian retorts while lifting Libby into her lap so my daughter can see.

"Actually, she was nine pounds three ounces and 23" long at birth.

I don't think Bella is quite there yet. I didn't get the opportunity to hold anyone this tiny." I smile at Adrian. "Liberty, this is mommy's friend Adrian." I point and Liberty smiles. "Adrian, this is my daughter Liberty. We call her Libby."

Adrian greets Libby, but my daughter is more interested in the tiny one in my arm. She points at Bella then looks up at Adrian. "Can you say baby? Baby?"

Libby shakes her head then extends her arms. I imagine she thinks Bella is a baby doll like the ones we play with most evenings.

"Libby go get your baby and show it to Adrian." She climbs down and toddles to her toy basket beside Alma's rocking chair. She doesn't show it to Adrian. Instead she plops down and proceeds to pull every toy out of the basket onto the carpet around her. Her short attention span allows me to talk to Adrian.

54

MADISON

"So, Hamilton doesn't know?" Adrian prompts, raising her brow.

I explain to Adrian the events that occurred after the bonfire party his last night in town. Then I share my fear the day I took the pregnancy test. "After my initial freak out, I realized if I told Hamilton I was pregnant he would give up baseball and takeover the farm in Athens." I glance down at Bella before I continue. "You know I'm right. There is no way he would have chased his baseball dream and I couldn't be the reason he gave it up. I plan to tell him. I planned to tell him this past winter, but he was so busy that Salem's wedding is the only time we could get together. I didn't want to take away from Salem's special day and I can't tell him over the phone. I wanted to let him settle into Major League Baseball so when I introduced Liberty to him, he would consider continuing his baseball career."

"Adrian, I love him so much it is killing me to keep them apart." I don't fight my tears. "He wouldn't have given it a second thought. He would have taken over his family farm so that he could provide the security and financial support we would need. Then every time he drove by the ballpark or watched a game on TV he would have resented me for getting pregnant. I just couldn't steal his dream from him." I wipe my tears as I clear my throat.

"Liberty turned one on March 10th. I was so excited when you gave birth to Bella two days before Libby's birthday. During all of our video calls when Bethany and you discussed your children growing up together, I longed for you to know about my daughter and realize our children are just a year apart."

Adrian wipes tears from her eyes. I know it is the post-partum hormones as my friend Adrian is too strong to cry. I know she hates feeling weak, so I ignore them.

"She's gorgeous. I love her curls and her dark eyes. And she has her daddy's height, too. There's no way anyone can deny she is Hamilton's little girl." Adrian pulls her eyes from Libby playing on the floor and returns them to me. "It's got to be hard looking at her every day and her reminding you of Hamilton while he is so far away."

I share with Adrian our love for watching Hamilton pitch during Cubs games. I tell her about the many video-journal clips I have created for him. I share how Alma assists me in caring for Libby while I am on the phone with Hamilton or the girls, how she cares for her when I must return to Athens, how her three children have adopted me as their little sister, and how I struggle every day to plan a time and way to talk to Hamilton.

"I've purchased a twelve-month calendar and keep it on my desk in my room. I asked Alma to ensure that I introduce Liberty to Hamilton before the end of the year. Each day I cross off knowing I am getting closer to the day I will tell him. He'll be done with his season in October. I will then have two months to make it happen." My tears return.

"Adrian, I've put it off for too long. I worry by delaying another year, I may hurt any chance I have of being with Hamilton after he meets Liberty. I've always intended to tell him. I only postponed so that he could settle in the MLB. I love him, and I want him to play baseball. I just couldn't take that away from him." Tears trail down my cheeks—I wipe them before they can fall on a sleeping Bella. I lift her tiny head, so I can place a kiss upon her forehead.

"He loves you, too." I lift my eyes from Bella in my arms toward her mother. "His kiss at Salem's wedding proves his intentions. He wants you." Adrian pauses to wave at Libby when she turns her way. "Did Hamilton share anything while the two of you were at his mom's? Any clues to how he wants the relationship to work?"

Liberty stands and toddles to me. "Dada?" She points at Adrian. My adorable daughter heard Adrian refer to Hamilton by name. "Dada?"

I extend my arm around her waist and lift her into the open side of my lap. "Yes, Adrian said Hamilton."

Libby waves at Adrian. "Dada…" She continues jabbering words that I have no idea what she is saying.

Adrian smiles at me. I tell her about the photos of Hamilton we keep visible and how we watch him pitch and point to him on the TV. With her short attention span, Libby slides down and turns to me. She says Alma's name and I let her know she can go find Alma in the kitchen.

While I look at Bella I answer Adrian's questions. "We didn't discuss a relationship, per se. He was very drunk when I got him home on Saturday. He barely made it to his bedroom before he began vomiting. He laid on the bathroom floor and got sick all down the front of him. When he took off his t-shirt it got in his hair. I had to undress him and put him into the shower. He was better after that, so I went to my room. I couldn't sleep. Hours later, I went to the bathroom and popped my head in just to check on him. He was awake and spotted me. Knowing how I struggle to sleep, he invited me to lay beside him." I shrug and sigh before I share the rest of the events from the next morning. Of course, Adrian asks for every detail when I confess we had sex again. Unlike her, I don't share in great detail.

"So, he laid that kiss on you in front of all of us to let us know he loves you. But he didn't plan out times for the two of you to meet, date, and stuff?" Now knowing all the details, Adrian seems as confused as I am.

Liberty runs into the living room announcing Alma's name. Alma follows her, places drinks on the coffee table, announces I have hogged Bella long enough, and steals her from my arms.

Later, as we eat a light lunch Alma prepared Adrian fake pouts across from me. When I inquire what's wrong she asks if Bethany has already met Liberty. I remind her Bethany's trip to Columbia was a surprise and I didn't plan for her to learn my secret before anyone else. I ask if Bethany knew Adrian was driving down today and she states she only told Winston at breakfast this morning. Good. I hope Bethany would have called to warn me if she knew what Adrian had planned.

Our afternoon together flies by. Adrian plays with Libby while Alma and I take turns holding Bella. Mid-afternoon Adrian leaves in order for her to arrive home before dark. At the end of it all, I'm glad Adrian surprised me today—I'm glad she now knows. Bethany and Adrian's reactions give me hope that Hamilton, his family, and my other friends will understand my reasoning when I introduce Liberty.

55

MADISON

My attempt to remain far, far away from Athens on Mother's Day weekend fails this year. I plan a day trip on Saturday to attend Troy's graduation from Athens Community College and Bethany's baby shower. When I agreed to attend, I informed my friends that I would not be spending the night —I claimed I wanted to spend Mother's Day with Alma when really, I plan to spend the day with my daughter. Of course, Adrian and Bethany know my real Mother's Day plans.

I recently developed a new addiction—I enjoy listening to audio-books of my favorite reads. After I read a book once and sometimes twice, I download it on Audible. I listen via my phone while I drive, clean, or lay in bed at night. On my drive to Athens today, I am enjoying Cambria Hebert's *Hashtag Series*. I've already read the series twice. My three-hour drive flies by as I enjoy the stories yet again.

I hit town twenty minutes before the graduation ceremony is slated to begin. I stop quickly to refill my gas tank for the drive home later today. At the college, I park along the street and slip into my saved seat with five minutes to spare.

Our gang does our best to embarrass Troy. Adrian blows her air-horn while the rest of us cheer loudly. Troy turns to the crowd points in our direction then raises both hands in rock-devil-horns while sticking out his tongue. Many in the crowd laugh at his antics. We on the other hand know we didn't embarrass him in the least.

Following the graduation ceremony, Troy and Bethany's family join us at the Christian Church for lunch and Bethany's baby shower. Their parents decided to combine the two celebrations into one event. Bethany's mother arranged for it to be at their church as it was one of the only venues big enough for both families and our group of friends.

Bethany looks amazing at seven months pregnant. Today I've seen first-hand the extreme level of Troy's overprotectiveness. Bethany shares new stories every time we talk, but seeing it live in person makes it more ridiculous. Bethany's parents drove her to and from graduation. Troy immediately places her in a chair, then waits on her hand-and-foot. She's only allowed to stand for her frequent visits to the restroom—even then Troy hovers.

I realize Bethany and Troy love spending time with their families, but this baby shower is out of control. I attempt to do a headcount but fail twice as people move around visiting and paying no attention to Bethany opening her two eight-foot tables full of gifts. If I average the two headcounts, there are at least forty people here. Young children run between chairs and tables unsupervised by their parents. Older relatives stand on one side loudly carrying on their conversation about The Farmer's Almanac's predictions for this summer, fall, and what it means for the crops. I struggle to focus on my friend and the reason we are all here at this moment. When their nearby conversation moves to recent deaths amongst their friends, I can take it no more.

"Excuse me," I interrupt as I approach their group. "This is Bethany's baby shower. Her *first* baby shower. I drove over three hours to be here today. This is not the time to discuss death and funerals loud enough they can hear you in the sanctuary. Please move your conversation outside or sit down and quietly watch Bethany and Troy open the baby gifts." I stomp back to my chair, throwing a glare over my shoulder. I dare them to defy me, but I hope

I didn't upset Bethany—she's the only one I care about. If anyone else didn't like my actions they can suck it. I want to celebrate with my friend.

When the elderly group grab their coats to leave, Bethany blows me a kiss before she returns to opening the baby stroller Alma and I purchased for her. It's the same model we use with Liberty as we walk McGee. I hope she enjoys it as much as I do.

Opening the baby gifts takes as long as Troy's graduation ceremony. Bethany rolls her neck and Troy massages her shoulders. She rubs her lower back and removes her ballet flats to wiggle her toes. I hope both families witness her exhaustion and leave soon. I hug Bethany and apologize for my outburst. Troy assures me I wasn't the only one annoyed. I inform Troy he needs to get her home in the next thirty minutes. She needs to put her feet up and be waited on for the rest of the day. I mention a massage would be a nice touch, too. I hug Bethany one more time, she whispers in my ear to hug Libby for her, and I leave.

56

MADISON

I know I shouldn't drive by. I already know her car is there, yet I find myself driving by the corner bar. Just as I thought. It's not even 4:00 p.m. on a Saturday and she is drinking. I'm not surprised she's here—I am only surprised by what I do next.

I park my car in the tiny gravel lot and walk into the Black Jack bar. The smell of stale beer and smoke assault my senses. My eyes struggle to focus in the dark space. The walls and ceiling are all painted black. The tables, chairs and bar stools don't match—some are even held together with gray tape. I easily spot my mother. She's leaning on the bar with a man on either side of her. The bartender and two men look my way as I enter. My mother doesn't bother turning her head.

Henrietta, the bartender, claims she's happy to see me back in Athens. I don't want her to get her hopes up. I don't plan to stick around. I won't be available for her to call to pick up my mother. That hasn't changed.

Even with Henrietta greeting me by name, my mother doesn't acknowledge my presence. I figure it's because she has already had too much.

I call to my mother, when she doesn't turn, I tap her on the shoulder. The man on her left places his arm out to steady her as she jerkily turns to look over her shoulder my way. Her eyes barely open and she speaks not a word.

"Just stopped in to say hello. It's been almost two years and I haven't heard from you. I'm glad to see you're not dead, nothing has changed, and you're still having fun. Guess I will stop by here to say hello in another two years." I hate my cold words.

I leave the bar and return to my car with my head held high and shoulders back. She doesn't define me. I am a good mother. I love my daughter. I'll never abandon Liberty the way my mother abandoned me years ago. I don't cry as I drive through Athens. I have no tears left for her just as she has none for me. I must be crazy to hope she will ever change. I was crazy to drive over here and go inside. It won't phase her, and she doesn't deserve my time.

I decide to treat myself hoping to change my mood before the long drive home. I purchase some cheese tots and a vanilla diet cola from the Sonic Drive-In. With a drink and a snack, I return to my audio book and head to the place I want to be most—Liberty is my everything.

57

MADISON

Our plan seems to be working. I limit my substitute-teaching to three days a week. Every day, I schedule me-time like showering or soaking in the bathtub, reading a book, giving myself a manicure or pedicure, doing things for me. Liberty greets me at the door each afternoon I teach. Her unconditional love and contagious smile bring light to my world.

On the days I don't teach, I attend counseling appointments then Liberty and I take a quick nap together enjoying our sleepy cuddles. With our naps I'm not tired all the time and still get a full night's sleep most nights. My depression meds are working. They make me feel like I'm living my life in a thick haze, but my new doctor likes the progress I've made. He claims we will adjust my dosage again soon.

Our evenings contain walks through the neighborhood, meals at the table, and a fifteen-minute break after every hour spent on work. With Alma's help, I better schedule my work and personal times. I will always need to work evenings and weekends to plan lessons or grade papers, but by balancing work and personal time, it seems easier.

It's a long uphill battle. I'm constantly struggling to swim against the current, but with the help of Alma and Hamilton I have the stamina I need. My days and nights contain more light than darkness now. With each passing week, the darkness continues to shrink. I can see a light at the end of the tunnel and I can fight this battle for me and for Liberty.

58

MADISON

I smile down at my sleeping daughter comfy in her crib. I tuck a wispy curl away from her closed eye. She plays at one-hundred miles per hour all day then crashes hard at nap and bed time.

My phone rings loudly from my bedroom. I turn off the lamp and pull the nursery door halfway as I return to my room.

"Hey, I thought you might be dodging my call tonight."

Hamilton's voice wraps me like a fleece blanket. I assure him I was just out of my room and not avoiding him. I sit yoga-style on my bed. I place my cell phone on two pillows in front of me, so I can relax my arms.

We chat about Hamilton's travel today and tomorrow's game in Arizona. I share about my week, teaching summer school and the many teaching positions I continue to apply for in hopes of securing a job for fall.

"Don't get too hung up on the job search," concern laces his voice. "Remember it's a numbers game. You should reward yourself for each one you apply for."

"Ham, I'm good. Really." I know he worries I might slide backwards. "I met with my doctor today. We've lowered my dosage for the second time. I'm on the lowest dose now. I still see my counselor twice each month. I feel good—I really do. I'm not trying to fake that I'm good for your benefit."

With Alma's help, I've mastered scheduling time for myself every day. I balance work, motherhood, and personal time. I continue to marvel at Alma's wisdom. I've started to fill a notebook with all the things I've learned while living with her.

"I believe you. It's just I know how excited you are to teach, and I hate that you haven't been offered a contract yet."

"About that..."

I'm glad Hamilton brought the topic up. I share that recently my work with Cameron and D.C. Bland Publishing I've enjoyed focusing more on my writing. Part of me feels guilty for seeking a degree in education and not using it to help children.

Hamilton states my young-adult books might help students experiencing similar situations. I'm using my degree in a different way. He claims when I earn my spot on the NY Times Best Sellers List I will reach more people than I could in a brick and mortar classroom.

I love that Hamilton supports my writing and possible career change. Sometimes I forget he is my number one fan.

"Why are you smiling?"

At my words, his sexy smile morphs into his patented smirk. Like it always does his smile, dimples, and dark stubbled jaw spark a fire in my belly while dampening my panties. My heartbeat quickens. I fight the urge to fan my overheated face aware that Hamilton can see me.

"You come alive when you talk about your writing. It's sexy."

"Sexy?"

Hamilton smirks but doesn't explain. My mind reels as my body continues to react to the words and sight of the man I love upon my phone screen. Hamilton quickly ends our call arousing my suspicion I might affect him as he does me.

I'm aware I won't be able to focus on writing or sleep until I remedy my current situation. Instead of fantasizing Hamilton in bed with me as I pleasure myself, tonight I imagine he's masturbating to thoughts of me while I masturbate to thoughts of him.

59

MADISON

In late-June during the last week of summer school, my administrator interrupts my class stating I have an important call. My mind races to Liberty with Alma and hundreds of horrible things that might have happened.

"I'll cover your class. I was told you need to check your cell phone."

I grab my phone from the outside pocket of my laptop case and dart from the room. My fingers scroll through several missed calls and texts from Alma, Adrian, and Salem. Once outside, I stop to read the texts in the order they were received. Bile rises in my throat, my legs give out, and I sit on the sidewalk.

"Adrian..."

"Madison, oh thank God, it's Bethany. Someone side-swiped her mother's car, her water broke, and she started having contractions." Adrian struggles to catch her breath through her tears. "Troy called on his way from St. Joe to tell me they were transferring her to North Kansas City Hospital. I can't remember what he said the reason was. I'm terrible at this, I'm sorry. I should have written everything down, but I was in shock. Madison, it's too early." Sniffles fill my ear. She can't lose this baby, too."

"Adrian," I firmly interrupt her hysteria. "She'll be okay. She's made it thirty-six weeks. Yes, it's early, but in Kansas City they see this more often." Through the phone, I hear Adrian's breathing slow. "It's a good thing they didn't keep her in Athens. The sooner she gets to the city, the better it will be for the baby. Now, is Winston with you?" Adrian states he is on his way home and Salem is on her way over, too. I ask about Bella and Adrian tells me she is napping.

"Okay, I'm going to stay on the line until Winston or Salem arrive. Honey can you go get a drink of water? Bella's going to need you when she wakes up." I try to distract Adrian from her frantic thoughts. I listen as she makes her way into the kitchen, opens the refrigerator, and guzzles from a water bottle.

"What now?"

"I don't know. I don't think I can drive to KC today. Alma's been with Liberty all day and I have to teach summer school for two more days. I'm sure Winston will drive Salem and you down, so the two of you will have to give me updates."

"Madison..." Adrian's faint voice pauses for a hiccup.

"She'll be alright. She's taken good care of herself. Both Bethany and the baby will be fine."

"Promise?" Adrian whispers. I hear the sound of a door in the background. Adrian calls to Winston. There's a muffled sound against the phone over which I can hear Adrian's sobs again. The sound against the phone grows louder.

"Madison," Winston's deep voice greets. "What can you tell me?"

I share what I was able to get from Adrian, which isn't much. I mention Salem is on her way to meet them. He tells me he'll drive the girls down to the city and he'll send me updates. I thank him, ask him to take good care of my girls, and to drive safely.

I take a moment to gather myself in the restroom. I lift a little prayer up for Bethany, Troy, and the baby. As I exit planning to return to class the final bell rings—classes are over for the day. I slowly make my way back to the classroom as students scurry out the door. With each day this week their excitement grows to begin summer like their friends.

On my drive home, my thoughts are on Bethany and Troy. I don't allow myself to think of them losing their baby. I need to be at home, holding Liberty in my arms until I hear an update from KC. I desperately need the comfort Alma and my daughter will provide.

60

MADISON

Hours pass. I busy myself playing in the back yard with Libby and McGee until storms threaten. Inside we play with building blocks and read several books. At 7:00 p.m. Alma encourages me to shoot a text requesting an update. I decide to send a group text in hopes that one of my friends has a moment to let me know if there is any update.

Me: anxious to hear if you have an update

Moments pass. I force the fear that attempts to overtake me back to the pit of my stomach. I ask Alma to keep an eye on Libby while I take a minute. I slip out to the back porch. A summer storm brews around us. Angry, dark clouds approach from the west, the winds pick up speed, and the temperature drops ten degrees. It would be easy to let this tumultuous weather influence my mood, but storms don't bring me down—they rejuvenate me. As a child, I thought I would like to be a weather-chaser and study meteorology. I've always been drawn to changes in the weather.

My silent phone in hand, I say another prayer. The wind picks up again and rain begins to fall from the oppressive clouds above.

"Mama," Liberty's soft voice calls from the screen door.

I turn to find her palms flat on either side of her face pressed to the screen. She's not smiling—she senses my mood. I open the door, scooping her into my arms and place a kiss on both her cheeks. I point to the clouds and rain while talking to her about the weather. I extend her fist over the railing of the porch allowing several sprinkles to wet her palm. Liberty squeals pulling her hand back giggling. As her mother, I love experiencing the world for the first time through her eyes. Libby extends her palm wanting me to help her catch the raindrops again. Her innocence and eagerness to explore lightens my heart.

When I place Libby on the kitchen floor while I latch the back door, she runs to the front room yelling for Alma. I smile knowing she babbles to share about the raindrops with Alma. Of course, she doesn't have the vocabulary yet, but she will continue as if we understand her. I follow behind her and share the raindrop story for Alma.

We bathe Liberty, place her in pajamas and each read a book to her before she finally falls asleep. Alma meets me at the bottom step with a glass of red wine. We settle in our favorite reading spots for the rest of the night. I understand my friends are scared, but with each half hour I don't hear from them my fears begin to replace my positivity regarding Bethany's baby. It's another hour before I receive a reply to my text.

Winston: it's a girl!
Winston: Bethany is fine, baby in NICU
Winston: Adrian will text soon

At the sound of the text alerts, Alma moved beside me to read with me. We breathe a sigh of relief. Alma fetches the bottle of wine from the kitchen suggesting we have another glass to celebrate before we turn in.

Later in my room, Adrian and Salem text me. They report Bethany is exhausted but healthy and happy. Salem calls me claiming it is too much to text. As Winston drives back to Athens, Adrian and Salem fill me in on speaker phone. Bethany's daughter is tiny and the doctors state she might be in the Neonatal Intensive Care Unit for a couple of days while her tiny lungs struggle to provide oxygen and she fights jaundice. She weighs 4 pounds 8 ounces and they haven't shared her name yet.

My girls report Troy is an even bigger mess now than he was during the pregnancy. He's torn between his daughter and wife's room. They have no idea how he was able to drive to the hospital when he left the police academy in St. Joe today. I explain he must have had his guardian angel on his shoulder the entire way and the girls agree.

Adrian shares Winston went to a nearby store for food and toiletries for Troy. He plans to decide in the morning if he can leave for the academy or not. He's much closer from the hospital than he is driving back and forth to Athens.

I claim I need to get to sleep so I can face my fifteen students in the morning. I thank Winston for driving my girls before we all say goodbye. I send a text about Bethany and the baby to Hamilton and inform Alma in her room before I turn off my light. With good news from KC and two glasses of wine in me, I quickly drift to sleep.

Over the next three days both Troy and Bethany text us photos and updates. Their daughter, Jameson or Jami as they will call her, improves every day. Troy continues to attend the police academy each day and spend his evenings with his girls. Bethany is discharged on the second day—her family secures a hotel room nearby for Troy and her to sleep in when they are forced to leave the hospital each day.

61

MADISON

As little Jameson begins day number seven in North Kansas City Hospital, an alert signals I have a text messages from Bethany.

Bethany: going home today
Bethany: Jami weighs 5 lbs this morning
Bethany: mom going to stay until weekend
Bethany: then Troy will be home
Bethany: please give us day or 2 to settle in
Bethany: then we will text/call u
Bethany: (heart emoji)

In the weeks that follow, Bethany continues her video calls to see Liberty. Now, I also get to see Jami during our calls. Bethany is the mother I always knew she would be. She's bubbly all the time. She makes her own wet wipes which probably means she will make her own baby food in the months to come. She even uses cloth diapers—

I cringe at the thought. As a stay-at-home mom she is able to spend much more time on parenting than I was. I am happy for her.

She continues to care for two other children during week days. She shares Troy loves the police academy and shares stories of bruises from handcuff training, as well as, the pain of pepper spray training. His training runs from 8-5 every week day. The toughest part is the three hours he spends on the road each day. He's committed to making it work for the 23-week course. Then he will wait two months for his twenty-first birthday to be eligible to work as a police officer. The Athens police department plans to give him more hours as a dispatcher while he waits. His dream is becoming a reality.

I'm happy that busy with his long days of training, Troy now enjoys time with his wife and daughter instead of his former overprotective ways. The new parents enjoy every moment of parenthood. Troy jokes about the long nights, dirty diapers, and spit-up. With large families nearby and frequent visits from friends Bethany and Troy overcame the heartache of a miscarriage and now have found their happily ever after.

62

MADISON

With summer school now over, I plan to enjoy my free time with Liberty and Alma. I still have no teaching contract for fall. Instead of continuing to apply for positions, I am focusing on my writing.

My work continues with Cameron and Bland Publishing. My first book will release next month with another to follow in September. The next two books are tentatively scheduled for January and April of next year. My unplanned venture into the world of an author is amazing. I find myself writing a bit every day often at night after Liberty falls asleep. I created a "To Be Written" Note on my phone that I am constantly writing new story ideas when they pop into my head and later enter them into my ideas notebook. While I continue to morph my previously written young adult stories for publication, I have new ideas for new adult and romance titles in my future.

My friends in Athens are crushing this adult thing. Winston and Adrian continue to run successful businesses while raising their beautiful daughter Bella. Adrian sneaks in a private video call from time to time while Winston golfs to catch a glimpse of Liberty and ask for parenting advice.

Salem loves her job as an LPN and helping Latham on the farm every moment she isn't at the hospital. She shared they are expecting a baby in February in our last text session.

Savannah continues to work fifty hours a week in the bakery. She offers to babysit on date nights for the other couples, while she seems to enjoy her single life. She and I are the only single ladies remaining in our group.

The ladies and I continue our Sunday evening video calls, but instead of weekly we talk on the first Sunday of each month. It's still only for us girls, but now Bella and Jami join us from time to time. Adrian and Bethany remain the only two friends that know about my daughter. Our friendships have strengthened by sharing parenting stories while they keep my secret.

The Chicago Cubs continue to have a record season. They currently lead the division by ten games. The World Series Talk grows more with each passing week. I hope this is the season I get to witness Hamilton pitch in the World Series. Alma, Liberty, and I watch every game Hamilton is on the mound. On nights he doesn't pitch the games are still on, but we listen more than we watch. Go Cubs!

Alma enjoys her busy life. We walk in our neighborhood and to the park. She is healthy and active in the church. My work with Cameron allows her to visit Alma more than ever before. Frequent visits from her three children and four grandchildren are her favorite times. With my help she's started video calls with her family and still joins me on mine with the girls in Athens.

The idea my college advisor had for me to live with Alma while attending college continues to prove advantageous for both of us. I would be lost without her guidance and help with Liberty. As our bond strengthens, I grow closer to my new adopted family. I can't imagine what my life would be like had I not met Alma. With her support I've completed my degree and, in a few weeks, will be a published author. Her time spent with Liberty eases my stress and saves me tons of money. She's introduced me to a supportive church family along with my new adopted siblings. My life is full because she's in it.

McGee and Liberty are best friends and partners in crime. They keep Alma and me on our toes both inside and outside the house. We enjoy our walks, playtimes, and frequent cuddles with both of them.

Hamilton and I continue to chat or text several of times per week. We haven't been together since Salem's late-December wedding, yet I think we are a couple in our own way. Hamilton now tells me he loves me and misses me during every call. He shares much more about his relationships with coaches and teammates and asks more details about my writing and new adopted-family. Although we live far apart we are closer than we've ever been, except for the gigantic secret part of my life I still keep from him.

Over the past two years my life took a different path than planned. It's not how I imagined life away from Athens—it's better in so many ways. I'm not sure what my relationship with Hamilton will be when I share about our daughter this winter. For now, I enjoy his distant love and presence in my life via our phones. It's not a conventional relationship, but I'm happy, hopeful, and it's all I have time for in my life right now.

The End
(For Now)
Madison's story continues in another Tailgates & First Dates.

TRIVIA:

1. Athens, Missouri is a fictitious town. There was once a township of Athens, but I could find no town.

1. The first and last names of *ALL* characters in this book are the names of towns in Missouri. (Except McGee the dog.)

1. Haley Rhoades is my penname. I created it using the maiden names 2 of my great-great-grandmothers on my father's side of our family.

ARE YOU SOCIAL?

Keep up on the latest news and new releases
from Haley Rhoades

Please consider leaving a quick review
on Amazon, Goodreads, and Bookbub.

ABOUT THE AUTHOR

Haley Rhoades' writing is another bucket-list item coming to fruition, just like meeting Stephen Tyler and skydiving. As she continues to write romance and young adult books, she plans to complete her remaining bucket-list items, including ghost-hunting, storm-chasing, and bungee jumping. She is a Netflix-binging, Converse-wearing, avidly-reading, traveling geek.

A team player, Haley thrived as her spouse's career moved the family of four eight times to three states. One move occurred eleven days after a C-section. Now with two adult sons, Haley copes with her newly emptied nest by writing and spoiling Nala, her Pomsky. A fly on the wall might laugh as she talks aloud to her fur-baby all day long.

Haley's under five-foot, fun-size stature houses a full-size attitude. Her uber-competitiveness in all things entertains, frustrates, and challenges family and friends. Not one to shy away from a dare, she faces the consequences of a lost bet no matter the humiliation. Her fierce loyalty extends from family, to friends, to sports teams.

Haley's guilty pleasures are Lifetime and Hallmark movies. Her other loves include all things peanut butter, *Star Wars*, mathematics, and travel. Past day jobs vary tremendously from an elementary special-education para-professional, to a YMCA sports director, to a retail store accounting department, and finally a high school mathematics teacher.

Haley resides with her husband and fur-baby in the Kansas City area. This Missouri-born girl enjoys the diversity the Midwest offers.

Reach out... she would love to connect with her readers.

amazon.com/author/haleyrhoades

goodreads.com/haleyrhoadesauthor

bookbub.com/authors/haley-rhoades

instagram.com/haleyrhoadesauthor

facebook.com/AuthorHaleyRhoades

twitter.com/HaleyRhoadesBks

pinterest.com/haleyrhoadesaut

tiktok.com/@haleyrhoadesauthor

linkedin.com/in/haleyrhoadesauthor

Made in United States
North Haven, CT
16 April 2024

51390922R00124